THE CROSSING

Alice Hepworth

BAD CREATIVE BOOKS

This book is a work of fiction. Names, characters, places and incidents are products of the author's imagination or are used fictitiously. Any resemblance to actual events or locales or persons, living or dead, is entirely coincidental.

ISBN 9798667132660

OTHER BADCREATIVE BOOKS

Banking On Love

The Jaguar King

Bewitching Amelia

Managing Complications In Anesthesia And Critical Care

Table Of Contents

<u>Chapter 1</u>

'College life is hell'. At least that was what Jonathan's older brother told him when he would start college. In truth, it was still his fourth day of college, but he was already feeling what most freshmen would feel. A sickness in his stomach. A sudden change in his routine. An unfamiliar environment and the impulsive need for a sense of normalcy. In short, he was feeling homesick.

He didn't have to worry of course. His parents and brother were just a phone call away. And his brother did go the extra mile in setting up his side of the dormitory. His brother had helped him mount posters of his favorite musicians like Dave Navarro, Black Sabbath, Sabaton, American Head Charge and Katatonia just to help him feel more at home. It still didn't help him with that all too familiar feeling of being away from home. But that didn't hinder him from his studies. So he plugged his headphones in his phone, set the playlist to that of Dave Navarro, turned on his study lamp, picked up his textbooks and began to study.

Cultural legends and beliefs of other societies. That was the topic for tomorrow's lecture with Dr. Lewis. He thought, as he highlighted the first few paragraphs of the chapter. He yawned for a bit as he wondered how this would apply in real life. Then again, understanding various legends and beliefs was something every sociologist needed to know. Especially in the age of social media and online forums, with stories that sounded much too impossible to actually happen.

He heard the door open. It was his roommate again. He thought as he focused on his textbook, reading under the light of the desk lamp while writing down notes on his notebook. He checked the time on his phone. 12:00 midnight! He went to another party! Jonathan groaned to himself. His eyes flinching as his roommate flipped the light switch on.

"God, Dick!" Jonathan groaned. "Think you can give a heads up when you turn on the lights?" He turned off his desk lamp, yanked his headphones out of his ears and glared at his roommate, Richard 'Dick' Berg, as he tossed his sweat drench shirt in the hamper and walked to his messy side of the dorm.

"Oh, hi Jonny." Dick replied. "Didn't realize you were studying, buddy."

"I thought it was obvious with my study lamp, headphones and open books." Jonathan often found himself asking why he was rooming with this stereotypical, frat party-going meathead who was more interested in getting high and going to parties, than actually going to class.

"Man, you Goth types really are buzzkills." Dick said as he put on a shirt from his closet, got on his bed and began texting on his phone. "And to think you're Alex Madden's younger brother. I thought you'd be just like him."

Yes, just like his older brother. Jonathan heard the same old tune playing. His older brother, Alex 'The Stampede' Madden. Famed quarterback and all-time college superstar. Famous for his continuous touchdowns during his second year, and president of the prestigious Sigma Chi fraternity. It was a legacy he left behind, but for Jonathan it was something he didn't want to be associated with. He was more content with being a hard rock loving academic, who had a thing for video games and pop culture. But when his brother dropped him off on the first day, it was clear to everyone who he was.

He didn't even like the idea that Dick viewed his brother as a role model of the ultimate college hero. He knew his brother better than Dick. Despite the image of a fraternity jock, his brother was just as responsible and devoted to his studies as any other student. Jonathan didn't mind the comparison too much, really. What he did mind was how Dick would call him a Goth.

"Just because I listen to hard rock and death metal doesn't mean I'm a Goth." He would say. But Dick was too invested with his phone that he didn't seem to hear Jonathan. That was fine. He thought to himself, as he placed his headphones on and went back to reading his textbook.

It had been a childhood dream of his to become a horror and mystery writer. Authors like H.P. Lovecraft and Stephen King were among his favorites. He knew that to be a good writer, he would need to understand various cultural legends and beliefs. With an understanding of human social interaction, he would be able to create stories like his favorite authors. And so, he decided to study sociology.

While he was still in high school, he would apply to various colleges, including his brother's alma mater, Berkeley. As if by luck, and probably via a non-divine intervention by his brother, he was accepted at the University of California, Berkeley's Sociology Department. He remembered coming home from school on the day the letter came. He remembered seeing the white envelope with the university's coat of arms, stamped at the top right corner. He remembered what he had felt when he saw the words "accepted at the Sociology Department's undergraduate program." It was like a dream come true for him. He wasted no time in preparing for his first day. And now, on his fourth day, he felt like all those stories he heard from various college graduates were starting to come true.

'You will be bombarded with assignments and lectures.' They said. 'Sleep will be a luxury for most students. You will learn to love coffee and energy drinks. You will be competing with other students.' They said. It didn't matter to Jonathan really. He would rather just pass through college and get started on his career path. It didn't matter if people recognized him as Alex Madden's brother. It didn't matter if he had a legacy to live up to, so to speak. He chuckled to himself, as he turned the pages on his textbook.

The next morning, Jonathan woke up and walked to the bathroom. He turned on the shower and felt the hot water flow onto his body. While some preferred cold showers to wake up, he would rather have hot showers to warm himself from the cold night. He soon walked out and took out a clean black shirt and pants. He found some socks and slipped them on before tying his shoes up. He noticed Dick was still asleep.

'I'd better wake him up'. He thought for a moment as he reached for his books and placed them in his backpack. 'Nah. I'll let him sleep.' He slung the backpack over his shoulder and walked out of his room.

A few steps away from the door, he noticed his neighbor, the French student, Milo Garnier leave his room. "Bonjour, Milo." Jonathan greeted. "Are you heading out to the cafeteria for breakfast?"

"'Ello, Jon." Milo replied in his heavy French accent. "Oui, I am going to have some petit dejeuner." Breakfast. Jonathan remembered his French. He liked Milo. In fact, Milo Garnier was one of the very few students who had no idea who his brother was.

Which was a reprieve of sorts for him. The two boys walked to the dorm's mess hall and lined up with the rest of the boys for their breakfast. "So, Jon. Are you free for Saturday?" Milo asked as they were served their breakfast of pancakes, jam, bacon and coffee.

"Sorry, Milo." Jonathan said. "I have an appointment with the dentist."

Ah...toothache?" Milo asked

"No, just a routine check-up." Jonathan touched his cheeks as he spread some jam on his pancakes.

"C'est la vie" Milo sighed. "A raincheck perhaps?"

"Rain check." Jonathan wasn't much of a social person even if he did like Milo. Still, he was somewhat glad that Milo understood. The two boys finished their breakfast, headed out of their dorm and walked towards the main campus buildings.

Jonathan liked walking to the campus. He liked to watch student life unfold in the college grounds. He would see students riding their bikes, students gathered in a circle, probably doing some club activity or playing the guitar, or even some students cramming while walking. However, if there was one thing he didn't like when he walked to the main campus, it was the fact that he would pass Greek row. As much as possible, he wanted to avoid the frat houses. He knew they would hound him to join their respective fraternities and it was something that was unavoidable.

"Hey!" He heard the first frat member of the day. "You're Alex Madden's brother, right? Wanna join us?"

Jonathan quickly walked as fast as he could; avoiding every frat member's persistent invitation. He wished there was another route to the main campus, but for now he had to deal with this. He made his way to the Sociology building and went to his first class.

He entered the classroom, walked to the back of the room and sat in one of the back seats. As he took out his notebook and pen, he heard a couple of girls sitting in the front row gossiping.

'Typical girl stuff.' He thought to himself. Then he heard one of them ask the others. "Have you heard of the Lady on the Horse ritual?"

Lady on the Horse? He repeated to himself. One of the girls replied. "You mean that fortune telling, wish granting ritual?"

"The very same." The girl replied. "You know that nursery rhyme, 'Ride a Cock Horse to Banbury Cross'?"

Ride a Cock Horse to the roads that cross

To see a fine lady upon a white horse.

Rings on her fingers and bells on her toes

And she shall have music wherever she goes.

Jonathan knew that rhyme. His mom often sang that to him when he was a little boy. He would often think of how the lady on the horse would look like. She's a beautiful lady with blonde hair and green eyes. His mother would always say. She wears beautiful clothes and jewels. She has bells on her ankles that jingle when she rides. He wondered why these girls were talking about an old rhyme.

"That sounds so lame." One girl said. "But how does the game go?"

The girl who opened up the topic said in a low hushed tone. "The Lady on the Horse is said to grant wishes and desires. If you want a wish to come true, you must go to a crossroad at midnight."

"A crossroad?" another girl repeated. "Like a particular crossroad? Does it have to be a crossroad called Banbury Cross?"

"No. Any crossroad where there are four directions." The girl replied "You must wait until the sixth stroke of midnight. That's when you'll hear the sound of bells and clip clopping hooves. You'll then see a beautiful woman on a white horse riding towards you. She'll have rings on each of her fingers and tiny bells on her ankles. She'll ask you what your wish is. You must tell her a wish. She will then give you one of her rings, and you must keep it with you until your wish is fulfilled. Once it's fulfilled, she'll come back and ask for the ring again."

"Why would she ask for the ring back?" One of the girls asked.

"I think it's like a loan of sorts." The girl replied. "Like she's letting us use one of her luck charms for the wish to come true."

"She won't ask for anything?"

"No." The girl leaned back on her seat. "But she's very selective with who she grants the wish to."

While the girls were talking, Jonathan was flipping through his textbook. This was the first he had heard of such a ritual game. It sounded like one of those made up games he would read about on the internet; similar to the elevator game, the window game and of course, the classic, Bloody Mary game. And yet, he was intrigued by this. Before he could say anything, their teacher walked in.

Dr. Joseph Lewis was a celebrated sociology and cultural researcher who had penned numerous articles and books; one of which was the very same book Jonathan was reading the night before. "Good morning class. Open your books to page 20, please." He said setting his bag down.

There was a collective sound of zippers being opened and books hitting the tables with delicate thuds before being opened. Dr.

Lewis had set up his laptop and had one of the students turn off the lights. A projector flashed onto the white board. "Can anyone tell me about cultural rituals?" he asked the class.

A few hands were raised. Jonathan kept his on either side. He would rather just listen instead of participate. After all, he would very much like to go through the semester without drawing attention to himself. Dr. Lewis picked one student. A Mr. Woods. "Cultural rituals are rituals that have significance to a particular country's culture?" He replied with an uncertain was-it-the-correct-answer tone. Jonathan just kept to himself as he wrote on his notebook.

"Anyone else?" Dr. Lewis asked. There were still hands in the air, but Dr. Lewis could tell that they were not sure of their answers. He then noticed a student dressed in black, sitting in the backrow, staring at his textbook with a blank and almost bored expression. He could see the student's attention was divided between his lecture and the group of girls sitting in front of him. "Mr. Madden, would you care to share what you can describe as cultural rituals?"

Jonathan looked up. Why did Dr. Lewis call him? He wasn't raising his hand. He wasn't ignoring the lecture. Was he trying to make a scene? Does he know he's Alex Madden's younger brother? What was it? Jonathan sighed and replied.

"Cultural rituals. Rituals by definition, are a sequence of acts involving gestures, words, objects or actions performed in a place and according to a set sequence. "

"Precisely." Dr. Lewis said. "You're Alex's younger brother, right?"

'And I was right to assume he knew Alex.' Jonathan thought to himself as he nodded. And he was so close to just breezing through this class without any mention of him being Alex's younger brother. He could see it now; they would be asking him about his brother, they'll be asking to spend time with him; hell, they'll even want to ask for Alex's number. But for some reason, Dr. Lewis didn't seem to do all that he had imagined. He just went on with the lecture.

"Cultural.... Rituals...." Dr. Lewis said as he highlighted the words on his virtual presentation. "By virtue, there are rituals that are well known among members of different cultures. One can even say it is part of everyday living."

"How so?" one student asked.

"A good example would be Japanese tea ceremonies." Dr. Lewis replied. "When they have guests or visitors, the Japanese would conduct tea ceremonies to establish a deep connection between themselves and nature. The steps like preparing the tea, whisking the tea and serving it in bowls all have deep significances."

A hand shot up in the air. Dr. Lewis looked. "Yes, Mr. Woods?"

"So what about urban legend games like Bloody Mary or the Elevator Game?" he asked "Would they be called cultural rituals?"

"They have no distinct cultural root, Mr. Woods." Dr. Lewis said. "Although they are somewhat well known in today's society, we cannot completely call them cultural rituals. They are simply rituals born out of fear of the unknown."

"So they don't work?" The student asked.

Dr. Lewis shook his head and resumed his lecture. Jonathan went back to writing down notes as he listened. He then heard one of the girls speak to him. "Hey, are you really Alex's brother?" she asked. Jonathan rolled his eyes and waited for the class to end.

****

As soon as the bell rang, Jonathan stuffed his notebook and books inside his bag and began to walk past the small space in the classroom. He was then cornered by the very same girls who sat in front of him. 'Great.' He thought to himself. 'I knew this was going to happen.'

"Hi." The first girl spoke. "We haven't been properly introduced. My name is Claire and these are my friends, Annamarie and Jane. You're...Jonathan, right?"

"Yeah." He replied nonchalantly. "Sure. Listen, I have to go to my next class."

"Yeah, we're in the same class." She said. "Want to walk together?"

"Nah. I kinda wanna do my thing." He replied as he quickly weaved his way out and walked out. He didn't like having these girls following or walking beside him. He knew the only reason they were interested in him was because of him being Alex Madden's little brother. He placed his headphones on and began to listen to Dave Navarro while walking along the hallway to his next class.

"Mr. Madden." He suddenly heard Dr. Lewis call him and walk towards him. He stopped for a bit and removed his headphones as Dr. Lewis stood in front of him.

"Dr. Lewis? Is there something you needed?" Jonathan asked, hoping he wouldn't hear his brother being mentioned in the conversation.

"You don't talk much in class." Dr. Lewis said. "And I was wondering what you intend to do after you graduate."

"Well…" Jonathan held the straps of his bag tightly. He had never before told anyone what he wanted to do after graduation. Then again, no one was really interested with what he wanted to be in life. They were more concerned about Alex and his many achievements. They were more concerned about whether he was going to follow in his brother's footsteps. "Well, Dr. Lewis. I was thinking of becoming an author. So, understanding sociology would help big time."

"I see." Dr. Lewis said, scratching his chin thoughtfully. "That is a very interesting career choice. Much unlike your brother, Alex. How is he?"

"Doing well." Jonathan shrugged. He waited for Dr. Lewis to make the whole brother conversation go even deeper. Any minute now. He thought to himself. But somehow, Dr. Lewis did not talk much about Alex after that.

"I'm looking for some applicants for my internship program." Dr. Lewis said. "Research assistants to be precise. And aside from allowance and travel opportunities, you'll have full credits for my course studies. Are you interested?"

"It is interesting." He said. "But why are you telling me this?"

"I liked how you answered my question in class." Dr. Lewis replied. "You were very sure of your answers. You didn't hesitate. I don't see that kind of conviction nowadays. Most students are only that focused for the sake of passing. But you're different." He took out a piece of paper and wrote his email down and handed it to him. "If you're interested, email me your resume." He then excused himself and walked away.

Jonathan watched the retreating figure of Dr. Lewis slowly disappear into the crowd before putting on his headphones and heading off towards his next class.

****

"Hey do you see that guy sitting at the back?" came the murmuring sound of girls as they whispered to one another.

"The one with the headphones?"

"He's Alex Madden's younger brother."

"No kidding. He's kinda cute don't you think?"

"I wonder if he's single."

"Better, what if he and his brother are both single?"

Jonathan increased the volume of his player, as he reached for another book from the pile of books he pulled out from the library shelves. He really didn't like unwanted notoriety and now this was happening. Even while he studied in the library, there was no escaping the gaze of the girls and fraternity boys.

Sometimes I wish I wasn't accepted at Berkeley. He would grimly think to himself. But at the same time, he was glad to be there. He remembered what his brother would often say. 'Just go about with what you're doing and you'll be fine.' Gee, that was easy for him to say. He thought to himself, when suddenly, he heard a thud as books hit the floor beside him. He looked to his side and saw a girl crouching down to pick them up. He took off his headphones off, got up from the chair and went to help her. "Are you alright?" he asked

The girl replied. "I'm ok. Sorry I didn't mean to bother you. My hands were getting sweaty from carrying all those books." Jonathan picked up one of the books and looked at the title. *LIBERTIE, EGALITE, FRATERNITE: The French Revolution and its Aftermath.* He looked at the other titles. *VICTORIA: The Young Queen who led an empire. The Outcome of the World's most Significant Wars. HITLER AND HIS CHILDREN: The Truth behind the Hitler Youth.*

"You're a History major?" Jonathan asked.

"Yeah." She replied as she placed the books on the table. "Artemis Rosi." She held her hand out.

"Jonathan Madden. Sociology major." Jonathan replied shaking it. He noticed her arm. She had a crescent moon tattoo with blue roses. He studied her from head to toe. She had brown wavy hair, olive skin and brown eyes. She wore black jeans, a blue shirt with a print of the famous Kanagawa wave design and sneakers. "Your last name...you're Greek."

"Kind of a dead give-away, huh?" she replied. "Yeah, I found out only last year that my last name meant the flower rose. So I decided to add that to my moon tattoo."

"Let me guess." Jonathan said. "An homage to your namesake, the Greek goddess of the hunt and the moon?"

Artemis chuckled. "Yep, the very same. That way, if anyone wants to know my name, all I have to do is show them my tattoo and let them guess." She laughed at her little joke. Jonathan chuckled as well. That was witty alright. "Hey, I hope you don't mind." She started. "There seems to be no more tables left. So, can I share your table?"

"By all means." Jonathan obliged. "Here, let me help you with those." He went and picked up the last of her books and placed them opposite his own pile. "Hey, don't look now. But I think you're being watched." Artemis pointed to a group of students sitting at several tables away from their table, their gaze completely directed at Jonathan.

He sighed and said as he sat on the table "Yeah it happens."

"That's kinda creepy." She replied sitting across him. "Unless I'm sitting with either a bully or a superstar."

"Not exactly." He shrugged. "I get this all the time because of my brother."

"Your brother?" Artemis repeated raising an eyebrow. "Why, what is he? Some kind of overpowered jock?"

"He was the star quarterback on the varsity football team." He replied, expecting a reaction from Artemis. There was silence. Any minute now. He thought. When she said nothing, he looked at her with a curious look. Was it possible that she had no idea who Alex was?

Artemis looked at him and asked. "Is he still enrolled?"

"No, he graduated two years ago." Jonathan replied.

"Oh. Well, good for him then." She began to drum her fingers on the books. "So why should that matter to you?"

"I sort of don't like being referred to as Alex's brother or the quarterback superstar's brother." He replied, explaining to her how he found it annoying every time he passed by Greek row. How it vexed him when the different fraternities would call out to him to join their house. How the girls would giggle and stare at him with flirtatious looks. "To be honest, it's kind of...unwanted attention that I don't need."

"So don't dwell on it." Artemis said. "The more you dwell on it, the more you'll be bothered. Besides, I'm sure sociology is a pretty tough major and you'll need all that energy in passing the subjects."

Jonathan chuckled. Artemis was the first girl who didn't seem to care whether he was Alex's brother or not. In fact, she was different. "Besides," She continued tapping his cellphone screen. "Any guy who listens to Dave Navarro is pretty much an interesting fellow." So she liked the same music he did. Jonathan was beginning to feel a bit comfortable with Artemis as they continued to sit in the same table. When it was time for his next class, Jonathan got up and excused himself. But not before giving Artemis his number and email. After all, apart from his roommate, Dick and neighbor Milo, he could do with a nice female friend or two. This was one of those moments when he would tell himself that he was glad that he got accepted at Berkeley.

<u>Chapter 2</u>

Claire O' Hara sat idly at her desk, staring at the blackboard while playing with her notebook pages and nibbling on her pen. She watched the other students write down the lecture in short form notes. How boring, she thought to herself. She looked over her shoulder and stared at the young man dressed entirely in black; wearing headphones and tilting his head to one side while he took down notes. He was brooding, quiet and handsome.

Like his older brother.

She didn't know who he was at first. But all it took was one remark from the teacher and she finally realized who he was. He was a Madden. Specifically, Alex Madden's younger brother. Her friends in the advance classes had told her how popular Alex Madden was with the other fraternities, and how skilled of a lover he was. She wondered if that statement held true for his little brother. But when she introduced herself to him after class, she was met with something that she never thought possible.

HE WASN'T INTERESTED IN HER.

This was completely new! She had never before been rejected by someone of the opposite gender. She was used to getting her man. Or at the very least, used to getting a man interested in her. But this man was different. And his indifference to the other girls only made him desirable.

"Girl." Claire heard her friend, Yvonne, say. "You're still gawking at him."

"Can't help it." She sighed. "He's really cute. They say his brother was as cute as any underwear model."

"Why are we talking about his brother all of a sudden?" Her friend, Anna said. "He isn't enrolled anymore in case you forgot."

"I know." Claire said. "But his little brother. And if he's Alex's brother, I bet he's good in bed."

"Seriously?!" Yvonne said, raising her eyebrow. "Is that all you could think of?"

"I'm sorry." Claire folded her arms. "But every girl needs a man to help her decompress after studying."

"I wonder who gave you that idea?" Anna said. "Besides, he brushed you off during Lewis' class. Maybe he already has a girlfriend."

Jonathan Madden having a girlfriend? That was impossible, Claire thought. There was no inclination that he had a girlfriend. "I'm sure he's just getting comfortable with his new environment." She said.

"He's not a dog, Claire." Yvonne said. Claire brushed off her friend's remark and focused her attention to the blackboard. She tried her best to listen to the lecture, but her thoughts were all on Jonathan Madden. Take away the black clothes and headphones and he would be a handsome heartthrob. Now if only he would look at her. She then heard some of the girls next to her talk about an all too familiar story.

"Did you hear about that third-year English major?"

"The one who won $50,000?"

"Yeah. I heard she played the Lady on the Horse ritual and asked for good luck and fortune."

The Lady on the Horse. Claire repeated the phrase over and over in her head. The Lady on the Horse who grants wishes. Wasn't she telling her friends this a few hours ago? Did it really work? She didn't want to tell her friends that she tried the game, but ended up waiting for nearly an hour. She was sure that it was one of those fictional stories people posted online just for kicks. There was no way it was real.

And yet, she couldn't help but think that perhaps it was real, and she was just not sure of what she wanted. If she tried it again, what would she ask for? She could ask for popularity. But that was already a guarantee for her since she was a member of one of Berkeley's well-known sororities. She could ask for money; her parents were not going to shelve out money for all the things she wanted like a new car, a new bag or even the latest iPhone. She could ask to become famous like her idols, the Kardashians. After all, they were famous for just being famous. Right? Or she could ask for the most handsome boyfriend in the world. That's it. She could ask for Jonathan. And the Lady on the Horse would give her that.

She immediately started to have fantastic thoughts of having a handsome boyfriend cater to her whims and wants. She would be the envy of every girl on campus. Even her own friends. As soon as class let out, she watched as Jonathan gathered his things and walked out of the classroom. She sighed, having visions of walking inside with his arm around her.

"Hello, Claire?" Her friends tried to catch her attention. But Claire kept on staring at Jonathan's retreating figure. She watched as he walked out of the classroom, his hands tucked in his pockets, and all manner of distractions obstructed by his headphones.

"Hello?" Yvonne snapped her fingers, effectively waking Claire up from her daydream. "What were you fantasizing about this time?"

"Wouldn't it be something if I dated Alex Madden's brother?" she asked, sighing in a wishful sort of way. "I'd be the envy of every girl on campus."

****

If there was one place that Jonathan liked most of all, it was the campus coffee shop. He loved the smell of roasted and ground coffee beans, and the satisfying sound of steaming hot brewed drinks being prepared by the baristas. More importantly, everyone was so focused on reading their books, that they wouldn't look up and stare at whoever came in.

That was perfect. Jonathan smiled as he walked inside the coffee shop and walked up to the counter. "Hi, guys." He said greeting the baristas.

"Hey Jonathan." One of the baristas, Ashley, replied. "What will it be?"

"Can I get a tall size, brewed coffee?" he asked. "One teaspoon of sugar and a little espresso?"

"The usual, huh?" Ashley said. "Funny thing, someone else ordered a tall size, brewed coffee with the exact same add-ons just a few minutes ago."

"No kidding." Jonathan said as he pulled out his wallet and paid for the drink. "Are they still around?"

"Yeah..." Ashley placed a tall cup on the counter. "Oh look, there she is." She pointed to a table by the window where a familiar girl sat reading. Jonathan looked over and smiled. It was Artemis. He then walked towards her and politely asked. "May I join you?"

Artemis, who had been reading a book while writing on her notebook, looked up and saw the towering figure of Jonathan standing before her, a cup of coffee in his hand. "Well, if it isn't Jonathan of the sociology department. "She smiled.

"Hello again, Artemis of the History department." He replied. "May I join you?"

"Sure." She replied as she gestured for him to sit opposite her. As he sat down, she took a whiff of his drink. "Hmm, I smell brewed coffee and...wait a sec, that smells like a teaspoon of sugar and a shot of espresso."

"I know." He replied. "The baristas told me you also order this combination."

"Really?" she asked. "That is a strange coincidence. I actually like it especially if I want to study and avoid my annoying roommate."

"You have an annoying roommate as well?" Jonathan asked. Artemis, seeing as this would eventually become a long conversation, closed her book and sat up. She held her cup of coffee and replied.

"Yeah. She's a bit of a party goer. Can't seem to study whenever she brings home her party mate."

"I get what you mean." Jonathan chuckled, thinking about his own roommate Dick. "Let me guess, when they come home, their speech is so slurred?"

"Exactly!" Artemis said, laughing. "I can't even understand why their parents send them to school if they're just going to be all attending parties and stuff."

"It's not our problem." Jonathan liked listening to Artemis as they talked about any topic they could think of: Studies. Annoying roommates. Family legacies. Hobbies, Favorite genres of music, etc. He was surprised to know that apart from liking Dave Navarro, Artemis enjoyed listening to electro and anything postmodern and vintage. In fact, he was starting to like Artemis.

"So, sociology major." Artemis began. "What do you know about fortune telling rituals?"

"Why do you ask?"

"Well a lot of girls are talking about this Lady on the Horse ritual." Artemis said. "If you ask me, it's all a bunch of hocus pocus."

"What makes you say that?" Jonathan asked.

"Because I tried the other fortune telling rituals like mirror gazing or even Bloody Mary when I was younger." She replied. "Nothing. But I'm wondering why they're talking about it."

"You know that rhyme of riding a cock horse?" he asked.

"Yeah, I had this nursery rhymes VHS tape when I was a kid." She replied. "Had something to do with riding a horse to meet a pretty woman in some place called Banbury Cross. But what does that have to do with the ritual?"

"I don't know." He shrugged. "But it is interesting. Say, are you free tomorrow?"

"That depends." She said as began to pack her books in her book bag. "Why, are you asking me out?"

"Well, there's this coffee shop in town that I frequent on the weekends." He replied. "They have live performances like poetry reading and musicians. I was wondering if you'd like to come watch."

"Are you doing a performance?" Artemis asked.

"You never know." He replied. She smiled and after a few minutes, both agreed to meet the next day. Jonathan then excused himself as it was getting late, and he needed to be back in the dormitory before curfew after all. "So, I'll see you tomorrow?" he asked, handing her the address to the coffee shop.

"Sure." Artemis nodded, slinging the straps of her book bag on her shoulder. "See you then." And she bade good bye and walked out of the café.

****

Artemis Rosi walked back to her dormitory building, her face bright red as though it were evident that something good happened. She opened the main door and walked up the stairs to her room. She walked in and saw her roommate had already started her nightly ritual of putting on her makeup. "Going to another party?" Artemis asked.

"Yeah, what's it to you?" her roommate said. "I don't ask where you're headed."

"You're right. Sorry." Artemis said as she carefully placed her bag on her bed and sat down on her desk. "I'm just gonna ask ahead what time will I expect you to come walking in, Claire."

"You don't have to wait up for me, Artemis." Claire O Hara said as she added some mascara. "Speaking of which, you look like something good just happened. Your face is all red and glowing and stuff…"

"It's that obvious?!" Artemis gasped, cupping her face on either side. Was it that obvious? Claire got up from her chair and Artemis could see that she Claire was wearing something that would not be out of place at a college party: corseted top, sandals, shiny shorts. She sat next to Artemis.

"Spill the beans, girl." She started. "Someone asked you out."

"It's not a date." Artemis protested. "And why are you being nice to me all of a sudden?"

Claire sighed and pulled out a tube of red lipstick from her make up pouch. "I keep telling my friends that my roommate is such a boring girl." Artemis raised her eyebrow. A boring girl? She repeated in her thoughts. Claire continued. "But I guess you're a regular Cinderella who just needs some fairy godmother magic. So here. Use this lipstick on your date tomorrow."

"It's not a date." Artemis said. "We're just going out for some coffee."

"That's a date, honey!" Claire said. "So use this lipstick and make sure you wear something really nice. None of that vintage thrift store stuff you wear."

"For the last time, it's not a-"

Artemis decided that it was somewhat pointless to argue with someone like Claire. In truth, Claire never really cared about her. In fact, she was slightly mortified at the idea that she would be roommates with someone like Artemis. But if there was one thing both girls were masters of, it was minding each other's business. Or simply put, they were civil with one another. They would exchange a friendly 'good morning' or 'good evening', and if either of the girls were feeling good, they would even offer a cup of coffee or a snack. But those were rare moments.

And this was a rare moment for her to be…friendly with her. If she weren't so vain and occasionally tactless, Claire would be a pretty decent roommate. Artemis thought. She saw that Claire was still holding out the red lipstick to her. "Do you really want me to wear your lipstick, Claire?" Artemis asked.

"Duh!" she replied. "Come on, let's see how you look with lipstick on." She unscrewed the tube of lipstick and began to apply a thin coat of lipstick on Artemis' lips. "And let's put your hair up." She fixed her hair up. She backed away for a bit and stared at her. "Oh my God!" she said breathlessly…

"What?" Artemis asked, sounding a bit worried at Claire's remark. "What is it?"

"Oh my god…you are a total hottie!" she replied. "Seriously, you're as hot and gorgeous as me." She then looked at the time. "Ok, we are going to finish this conversation when I get back, okay?"

"Assuming I don't fall asleep after studying." Artemis said.

Claire reached for her handbag and headed out the door. "Whatever, girlfriend. We'll continue when I get back. Bye for now."

Artemis raised an eyebrow. Since when did Claire start getting all friendly and stuff?

Meanwhile, Jonathan had only started to finish his chapter on the cultural norms of the ancient world, when he heard the door of his dorm open. He smelled the familiar cologne of Dick, his roommate. He's early. He thought, as he checked the time on his phone. 8:00pm. Or maybe not. Just then, Dick pulled Jonathan's headphones off. "Hey!" Jonathan said as he stood up. "What the hell, Dick? I was listening to that."

"Dude, I just heard something really interesting and you better confirm it with me." Dick said, setting the headphones down on the desk. "You're going on a date with someone aren't you?"

"Who told you that?" Jonathan asked.

"I knew it!" Dick exclaimed as though he had won the grand prize. "So it's true. Alex Madden's little brother has a little girlfriend! And here I thought you were a creep."

"Who told you I was going on a date?" He asked again.

"The baristas when they were clocking out." Dick said as he opened his closet. "I'm dating one of them." But of course. Jonathan thought. Dick, the party animal. "So, who's the girl?" Dick asked.

Jonathan took his headphones back and placed them on his neck. "None of your business." He replied. "Besides, why should you care?"

"I care, because you're my roommate and by extension, my responsibility." Dick said. 'In whose warped world, I wonder.' Jonathan thought to himself. Dick then sat down on the desk' table top and said. "It's cool if you won't tell me. But at the very least tell me where you're taking her."

"Just a coffee shop off campus." Jonathan replied. "The one under another shop."

"Oh, the beatnik place?" Dick said as though Jonathan said something…uncool. "You're taking her to the place where all loners and artists gather?"

"They have good shows." He replied. "You should stop by sometime. And besides, it'll give me a good excuse to use the scooter Alex gave me."

Dick sighed and went back to looking for a shirt. After selecting a red shirt, he told Jonathan that he would be back after midnight and headed out. Jonathan let out a sigh of exasperation as he turned on his playlist and resumed his reading. All the while thinking about what Artemis asked him in the coffee shop. And what those girls in Lewis's class were talking about. The Lady on the Horse……

****

The music was loud and the drinks were endless at the many parties that occurred on that particular night. Claire took another shot of vodka while checking her phone for the time. 11pm. There was still an hour left, and she was still not as drunk or as entertained as usual. Still, that didn't dampen her mood. She was just passing the time. After all, she was not about to wait for an hour or so at a crossroad for some lady on a horse.

"Hey, why are you checking your watch?" she would hear one of her friends ask as she drank her cup of booze. "They're bringing in an electric bull……An electric bull." Her speech began to slur, indicating that she was getting drunk.

Claire looked at her watch. 11:20pm. She took out her phone and began to search for the nearest crossing. A place where all the four directions met. She found one just a few blocks away. She checked her watch again. 11:30pm. She only had 30 minutes before 12 midnight. She watched as her friends began to enjoy themselves. She could easily slip out of the venue, grab a cab and go to the crossing.

And that was what Claire did. Quietly, she slipped out of the venue and into the street. She looked for a cab. 'Were there any cabs at this time?' She asked herself as she checked her watch. 11:35pm. She was starting to get frantic. She had to get there before midnight. As if luck would have it, a cab came cruising down. She quickly hailed it and got in.

"Where to, miss?" the cab driver asked.

"To this address!" She replied, dictating to the driver the address. The driver raised his eyebrow in complete bewilderment. He looked at her through his rear-view mirror. Why did she want to go there at this time? 'As long as she pays', he thought as he started the meter and began to drive.

They drove along the seemingly empty street, watching the crowd and cityscape. Claire checked her watch. 11:46pm. She then checked her phone. They were still a few blocks away. She couldn't be late. Thinking quickly, she tapped on the glass that separated her from the driver.

"Excuse me." She said. "Could we go a little faster? I need to be there before 12 pm."

"Miss, if I go any faster, I might get a speeding ticket." The driver said. "And I'm not about to have this cab impounded just for that."

"I'll pay extra." Claire said. "So, please!"

The cab driver shrugged in utter confusion. Then again, she was going to pay extra. "You're the boss." He said as he started to drive as fast as ever. The cab wove through the streets, taking care not to hit any crossing pedestrian. They arrived at the destination. Claire paid the driver and got out. "Be careful out there, miss." The driver said, sticking his head out of the window. "It's not safe during the hour." And he drove away.

Claire walked along the road and came upon what looked like a crossroad. She saw that each of the directions pointed towards a long, dark road. She looked to the front and back. She looked to the left and right. Completely pitch black. She walked to the center of the crossing and checked her watch. 11:55pm. Only 5 minutes. The cold night air began to blow and she could see the leaves rustling around in small circles. She shivered from the cold air and started to wish she had worn something warm. Or at the very least brought a cardigan with her. She looked at her watch. 11:59. Almost midnight. She thought about what she wanted to ask.

Should she still ask for Jonathan Madden? He was of course handsome and it would make her even more popular if she dated Alex Madden's brother. Or maybe she could ask to be accepted in Sigma Kappa. That was the University's most popular sorority. Or she could ask to be popular and famous. Like all those Youtubers and Instagrammers.

She looked at her watch. It was now 12 midnight. She heard it sound off. One.... Two.... Three.... Four.... Five.... Six. ......Silence. At that point, there was a strange sound coming from her right side. It was faint at first, but they were drawing near. She listened carefully. It sounded like.... the clip clopping hooves.... of a horse! She turned her attention to her right. Her eyes widened with both awe and disbelief.

Trotting towards her was a large white horse with large hooves and long trusses of blonde and white hair. It had beautiful, obsidian eyes and a smooth, velvet like pelt. There was a fine leather saddle that had little jewels that shone like stars, mounted on its back. And sitting on the fine saddle was a woman. Claire tried to take a good look at the woman, but she couldn't see her features clearly. The woman was dressed entirely in white with white and gold silks draped over her body. There was a white veil that covered her face, save for her eyes, which were a beautiful shade of amber, and a few strands of red hair peeked out from the silks. On her fingers were rings of different shapes and jewels, and on her wrists were gold and jeweled bangles. There were gold anklets with large bells that circled around her ankles. As the woman and the horse drew near to Claire, the sound of the twinkling bells pierced through the stillness.

It's her. Claire thought to herself. The Lady on the Horse. "She's real." She said in a soft whisper as the Lady on the Horse slowly approached her and stopped in the middle of the crossroad.

Claire looked at the Lady; even if her face wasn't quite visible, she could tell that she was beautiful. And the horse was tall and large with an eerie and gentle look in its eyes. She took a deep breath and said. "Are you the Lady on the Horse?"

The Lady did not reply. Claire wondered if she was doing it properly. She took another deep breath and asked. "Are you the Lady on the Horse? Can you grant me my wish and desires?"

The Lady then looked at Claire and began to speak in an almost ethereal tone. "What do you desire?"

Claire had thought about what she wanted and she knew exactly what to say. "I want to be rich, famous and adored. So much so that even the most desirable bachelors would want me."

"Why do you wish for that?" the Lady asked.

"I want to be desirable." Claire said. "I want to be as famous and desirable as any woman in history. I would give anything for that."

The Lady was quiet. Then she reached for her hand and pulled out a ring with diamonds around a large ruby from one of her fingers. She gestured for Claire to present her ring finger to her. The Lady slipped the ring on and said in a low and soft voice that only Claire could hear.

"Wear this ring and your desires will come true. And when you are satisfied with your desires, I shall come and collect this ring once more."

"Why will you collect the ring?" Claire asked.

"It is a favor." The Lady replied softly.

"That's it?" Claire said. "So, I don't have to do anything else? I don't have to make an offering or something?"

The Lady on the Horse said nothing, but there was a glint in her eyes that seemed to say otherwise. She and her horse then trotted onwards before disappearing into the darkness, leaving Claire all by herself at the crossroads. Claire looked at the ring, smiling with glee, wondering whether her desire and wish would actually come true.

<u>Chapter 3</u>

Jonathan stared at himself in the mirror as he smoothed out the small creases of his shirt. He picked up his comb and began to comb his hair. Dick watched as Jonathan got ready and began to snicker. "Hey, Jonny. Looking good. Are you going out on your date?"

"Haha, very funny, Dick." Jonathan said.

"You want some cologne?" he asked. "I got some Old Spice that you can use."

"Nah, I'm good." Jonathan politely refused. "Besides, I have my own cologne."

"I still don't get why you won't tell me who your date is." Dick frowned.

"'Cause it's none of your business." Why should I even tell you, Jonathan thought in the back of his mind. He set the comb down and picked up his backpack and keys. He opened his closet and pulled out two helmets.

"Jonny, you'll need this." Dick said as he stood up, walked over to Jonny and placed a small foil packet in Jonathan's hand. Jonathan looked at the packet, and frowned at Dick as he tossed the packet back at him.

"Thanks, but no thanks." He said. "This is not a date. It's something I invited her to. And I'm not taking that with me."

He then bade goodbye to Dick, walked out of his room and headed out of the dorm. He walked to the back-parking lot of the dorm and unclipped his scooter. He fastened one helmet on and inserted his key into the ignition. He started the scooter and sped along the vast campus grounds. He was surprised to see that there were several light gray clouds forming in the sky.

'Looks like it's gonna rain.' He thought to himself. He was somewhat glad he had brought an extra raincoat just in case. Just then, little droplets of water started to fall on his face. It was raining. He found Artemis sitting on a bench by the steps of the library. She held a pocket umbrella in her hands which shielded her from the rain. He stopped by the sidewalk and waved to her.

She saw him and walked over to the scooter. "Wow, I didn't know you had a scooter." She said.

"What? Did you think we would walk all the way?" he chuckled as he held out the extra helmet to her. Artemis folded her umbrella, took the helmet and sat behind Jonathan on the scooter. "Hold on tight, okay?"

"Come on, Jonathan." She said. "This isn't my first scooter ride."

He looked over his shoulder and at Artemis. He smiled and then drove along the wet road. They entered the main street and passed several shops and buildings. Jonathan then stopped in front of a brick cladded building with black iron railings. After parking his scooter, he and Artemis made their way towards the building where a set of stairs led to a door underground. There was a neon lit sign shaped like a mug with steam coming out hung next to the door. The letters on the sign read 'UNDERGROUND BREWS.'

"Underground Brews..." Artemis read the sign. "Clever use of word play."

"This way." He said as he unzipped his jacket and shielded both of them from the rain with it. They made their way down the stairs and entered the underground coffee shop. The moment they closed the door behind them, there was a warm, permeating smell that first greeted them. It was the smell of freshly roasted coffee beans and hot, freshly baked pastries, that were displayed on baskets and racks. The walls were exposed bricks with different framed pictures and posters depicting local celebrities, events and even popular coffee shop sceneries. There were small tables and dark leather chairs and booth seating all around. There were even some leather sofas and low coffee tables. In the center of this underground coffee shop was a small stage intended for live performances.

The pair noticed that there was a fair number of customers inside. 'Must be because of the rain,' Jonathan thought as they walked to the counter and ordered their drinks. Once they got their drinks, they wove their way to a small booth seat and sat down. Artemis held her drink in her hands and took a quick sip.

"Wow." She said. "This is delicious. How come I haven't heard of this place?"

"Well..." Jonathan began, taking a sip of his drink. "My brother told me about this place when he was still in college. He said that if ever I wanted to get away from all the hum drum of college life, this was the place to go to."

"That's smart of him." She replied. "Gosh, I have never been in a ...beatnik place. If you catch my drift."

"Yeah." He looked around and then back at her. "I may like Dave Navarro and Katatonia, but that doesn't mean I don't like other genres of music. And when it comes to coffee shops and the rainy season, nothing beats lo-fi music."

Artemis chuckled as the aforementioned lo-fi music began to play around the café. She then looked at Jonathan and said. "So, why did you ask me here?"

"I figured you would want a break from all the annoying stuff we talked about yesterday." He replied. "Speaking of which, you look really nice today." He hadn't noticed it at first, but apart from the slightly wet jacket that was now drying on the chair, Artemis was wearing a white eyelet lace top, blue jeans and blue shoes. Her hair was up and she was wearing light red lipstick.

She laughed uneasily and said. "I was ambushed by my annoying roommate. She said that I couldn't possibly go out looking like me so she starts, and I quote her, giving me a fabulous makeover."

"My roommate tried to pull the same stunt on me." He said. "Even went as far as letting me use his Old Spice and giving me a condom."

Artemis laughed at that and replied. "Who uses Old spice anyway? And besides, what's wrong with two people just hanging out and having fun?"

"Right?" Jonathan said. "I mean, there is no sexual connotation in two friends just enjoying a cup of coffee and good music." He stopped for a bit. Did he actually say sexual connotation? Was it slightly implying? Truth be told, he liked Artemis as a friend. But he was beginning to see her in a different light.

Don't rush into it, Jonathan. He told himself. She's your friend. "Hey Jonathan…" Artemis' voice cut through his thoughts. "Do you remember me asking you about this ritual some girls were talking about?"

"The Lady on the Horse, right?" he asked. Why was she asking him that again? Was there something about the ritual that was bothering her? "Why do you ask?"

"My roommate came home this morning at 2am." She replied. "I was awake because I had this homework on the Seven Wonders of the Ancient World. Anyway, she came home and she looked as if she won the lottery or something."

"Maybe she did." He said. "So how is that connected to your question about the ritual?"

"She was talking about it for some time now." Artemis replied. "When she came home, she didn't look like her usual self."

"Meaning?"

"When she goes partying, she's usually so wasted that the moment she goes through the door, she passes out on the floor." She explained. "Usually, I'm the one who drags and puts her to bed. But instead, she walks in…completely sober and looking like a million bucks."

"I guess something good happened to her." Jonathan said as he drank his coffee. "My roommate is sort of like that when he gets in sober."

"Maybe." She said. "But it is weird though. She has been talking about this ritual, so I tried looking it up online. Apparently, a lot of people claimed that it works and things have improved for the better for them."

"Are you tempted to try it?" he asked.

Artemis shook her head immediately. "No. Because if there is one thing that is common with ritual games like that, it's that everything has a price. And sometimes no one knows what the price is until it's too late."

He had to admit. She did have a good point about ritual games having prices of sorts. After all, in his reading about cultural rituals, every step of the ritual had specific significance. He recalled Dr. Lewis's lecture and how he used the Japanese tea ceremony as a definitive example. Each step like grounding the tea, whisking the tea and serving it in bowls all had some significance.

If that were the case, what significance did this Lady on the Horse ritual have, and exactly what kind of allure did it have on those interested in doing the ritual.

Jonathan then heard Artemis recite a few lines from a particularly familiar nursery rhyme. "Ride a cock horse to Banbury Cross.... to see a fine lady upon a white horse..."

"Are you reciting that rhyme?" he asked as they finished their drinks. "If I remember correctly, the next line goes like this. 'rings on her fingers and bells on her toes. And she shall have music wherever she goes."

"I'm sure there must be some historical facts to that." Artemis said. "And somehow, some idiot twisted it into an online ritual game. I personally don't think it's real. But you know what they say about the human mind..."

"What do they say?" he asked.

"The mind's perception is so strong that it can even defy the laws of reality and physics." She replied. "And in that aspect, it's something really scary."

"What do you say we find out the history about this Lady on the Horse ritual." Jonathan asked.

"Huh?" She looked at him with a puzzled expression.

"You're into History. It will be fascinating to find out stories behind certain things." He explained with a rather inquisitive look in his eyes. "And as a sociologist, it will be interesting to understand why it attracts modern society."

"Are you suggesting we treat it like...a.... like a project?" she asked.

"Why not?" He said. "It would be fun. And besides, it would give us both an excuse to avoid our annoying roommates every now and then." Artemis laughed and he laughed himself. They continued to enjoy their coffee until they heard the rain slowly subside.

After Artemis thanked him for the coffee and the enjoyable time, Jonathan drove her back to her dorm. As she got off from the scooter and handed him the spare helmet, she leaned forward and kissed his cheek. Jonathan blushed a bit after she did. He had never had a girl, apart from his mom, sisters and female cousins, kiss him on the cheek.

"It's a thank you for the great time at the coffee place." She said, turning red herself. "Well, I'd better get in or else the rain might get worse." She waved goodbye and hurriedly walked back to her dorm.

Jonathan revved up his scooter and sped along the wet roads. He was passing by a shop with large windows, when he noticed a strange image being reflected as he passed by. Out of the corner of his eye, he saw what looked like the image of a woman dressed in white and sitting on a large white horse. He stopped for a bit and looked back. The shop window showed no other reflection, save for the customers and the shop's products.

He wondered about what he had just seen. He was sure he saw a woman on a horse. Specifically, a beautiful looking woman on a large horse. He quickly brushed it off, thinking that all that talk about a fortune granting ritual and an old nursery rhyme was getting to him. He approached his dorm and parked his scooter in the parking lot before walking inside. He ran into Milo, who had picked up a large box wrapped in brown paper.

"Bonsoir, Jonathan." Milo greeted. "Zut alors! Why are you wet? Did you not know it was raining earlier?"

"Yeah." Jonathan replied, noting his drenched jacket and still wet hair. "I was at the coffee shop in town."

"With a girl, I hear." Milo added enthusiastically. 'Oh great,' Jonathan thought. Milo must have heard it from Dick. After all, it was typical of someone like Dick to tell everyone what he felt was a great event. And the younger brother of Alex Madden going out with a girl was a great event. Luckily, he knew just how to handle this kind of conversation. Milo then continued. "So, who's the lucky girl? How did the date go?"

"First, it wasn't a date." Jonathan said. "Second, it's no one's business as to who I was seeing or what I was doing. It was a nice coffee get together. Nothing more." He climbed the first three stair steps. "If you will excuse me, I'm going to shower before I get sick." He noticed the package in Milo's arms. "I'm assuming that's from your folks back home?"

"Oui'" He replied. "Ma mere' has sent me some of my favorite 'collation francaise'. I was feeling.... how you say...... 'le mal du pays'.... sick of home?"

"Homesick." Jonathan said. "Well, enjoy your parcel. I'm heading up." He climbed the stairs and went to his room. He closed the door behind him, only to be ambushed by his roommate, Dick.

"So, how did it go?" he said in a booming voice. "Did you do her? Did you kiss her? Did you get her number?"

"Hey, what gives!?" Jonathan said. "What's got you all worked up?!"

Dick reached around and locked the door behind him. "Tell me how your date went!"

'Sheesh! What is with this guy?' He thought to himself as he walked to his closet and pulled out warm and clean clothes. "Dick, why are you so interested in what I do in my free time?"

"Come on, man!" Dick whined. "We're supposed to be bros!"

"Funny, I don't remember making that agreement." Jonathan said as he walked to his hamper and began to remove the damp clothes. Dick sat on the bed and sighed heavily. "Come on Jonny. I bet like $50 that you at least kissed her!"

So that's what it really was. Jonathan sighed. Typical. "And exactly how much is at stake here?"

Dick quickly began to use the calculator in his phone. "I bet $50 that you kissed the girl. The rest of the boys each bet $60 that you didn't. That's $350 at stake! Come on Jonny. If you did kiss her, I win the $350. But if you didn't, I'd have to pay the boys $50 each!"

"Technically, she kissed my cheek." Jonathan said. "But, I don't- "

"Works for me!" Dick said, jumping out of his bed and bolting out of their room. "$350! Here I come!"

'Even a guy like Dick deserved a little bit of joy once in a while.' Jonathan thought, as he picked up his towel and went to the bathroom to shower. He turned on the shower and stepped in. He felt the warm, refreshing drops of water splash on his body. It was cleansing and hot at the same time. He could see the steam slowly rise and cover the entire bathroom. He turned off the shower and began to scrub himself with soap. He could hear the tiny drops of water drip down from the shower head and hit the floor. It was a soothing of sorts. If it were any louder, it would almost sound like the clip clopping sound of hooves.

'It does sound like clip clopping hooves.' He thought to himself. Wait! Why am I suddenly hearing clopping hooves? It's just dripping water. He turned on the shower to rinse off the soap from his body. He could see the steam slowly fill the room up once more. He scooped up some water and splashed it on his face. As he opened his eyes, he saw a strange silhouette across the blue plastic shower curtain.

It looked like a tall woman dressed in a long dress or robe. He could see what looked like two small red dots where the eyes ought to be, and long hair that seemingly reached to her back.

"What the?" Jonathan said. He reached out to open the shower curtain. "Who's there?" He called out, drawing the curtains open.

There was no one there. Confused, Jonathan turned off the shower, wrapped the towel around his body and looked around the bathroom. It was practically empty. He looked around the dorm room. The door was closed and the windows were bolted shut. There was no way that someone could have entered the room and left without opening either the door or the windows.

So what was that just now?

Jonathan opened his closet and changed into some clean clothes. He brushed it off as another product of an overactive imagination like his. After all, all this talk about the Lady on the Horse ritual was slowly getting to him, it seemed. He sat on his desk and opened his notebook to work on his homework. All the while thinking about the kiss on his cheek and Artemis's smiling face.

****

Artemis sat on her desk as she dried herself off with a towel. She opened her laptop and began to work on her History homework. She wondered where her roommate had run off to. "Probably partying the night away." She said out loud. She had just picked up her book and began to read the first few chapters on the book, when she heard the dorm door open.

Claire's back. She thought to herself as she saw Claire walk into their dorm room. "Oh, you're back early." Claire said. "So, how did the date go?"

"It wasn't a date." Artemis replied. "We just had coffee at his favorite coffee place."

"That is literally a date!" Claire said as she sat on a chair next to Artemis. "So, did you guys kiss?"

"Well, I sort of kissed him on the cheek." She said, feeling a bit embarrassed. "He really showed me a good time."

"Ooooh!" Claire squealed, literally jumping off her seat. "You like him don't you!?"

Why was this girl so interested in what she did? Artemis thought. But at the very least, she wasn't as overbearing as before. Or as insulting as when they first met. She then noticed a rather luxurious looking ring on Claire's finger. It had a large red ruby that was surrounded with small diamonds. The ring looked expensive. She thought. And she knew Claire never had a ring as expensive looking as this. Maybe it was given to her. Or maybe it was something she bought for herself.

In fact, now that she could see Claire up close and personal, Artemis could see that Claire looked like she'd had her hair done in a salon and was wearing what looked like branded clothes. Her nails looked well-manicured and polished with bright red nail polish. Her face also looked smooth and fresh; like she had gone to a skin clinic or spa. There was also the fact that Claire looked like she had won the lottery. At least, she won again.

"You're looking a lot...chipper." Artemis said. "I take it something good happened?"

"Oh." Claire said. "Well you know how it is. Good things happen to popular girls." I had to ask. Artemis sarcastically thought as Claire continued on to tell her about the amazing day she had, "So I was just getting out of class and getting a drink at my favorite smoothie place. I ordered my usual smoothie and then I'm told I won an all-expense paid trip to the spa!"

"Wow that is lucky." Artemis said.

"I know, right?" Claire went on to tell her about how she won an instant cash prize, how she was scouted by a modeling agent and so on. "I just had an amazing day and I'm sure there will be more to follow."

More to follow? Artemis thought. Claire then got up and decided to go out and get some food. She asked Artemis if she wanted anything. She politely declined, stating that she had eaten before. Claire walked out of the dorm as Artemis plugged in her headphones to her laptop. She resumed her History studies and opened her book. She flipped through the chapters until she came across a chapter with an image of a woman riding on a white horse nude. A small caption read: Godiva, Countess of Mercia.

She knew the legend of Lady Godiva and her well known ride to persuade her lord husband to alleviate taxes, following the latter's conditional request for her to strip naked and ride along the streets on a horse. So, on the next day, Lady Godiva rode to a crossing on the streets of Coventry and began her famous ride.

Lady Godiva was indeed a fine lady. Artemis thought. But that was entirely different. The Lady on the Horse was said to be dressed in fine clothes, while Lady Godiva had stripped herself of said fine clothes. She then flipped the pages and found another chapter with a photo of a woman dressed in angelic clothes, with a long white cape, and sitting on a horse. The caption read: Inez Mulholland.

This one, she knew just recently. She was a wealthy woman who was the spokesmodel for the Suffragists movement whom they called 'the Suffragists' Joan of Arc.' Another lovely lady riding a horse, and leading a parade from a crossroad in Washington.

Artemis could see that these two women, although different in background, possessed similar traits in their popular portrayals. Both were fine women and both rode horses. Both of them could have easily contributed to the ritual imagery. But what about the old rhyme?

She chewed on the tip of her pen as she thought about the rhyme. How old was this rhyme? While she read and researched, she suddenly noticed a figure passing by her window from across the street of her dorm. It was faint and somewhat distorted due to the rain, but she could somehow make out its shape.

It looked like a slender hooded figure dressed in white, and riding a horse on the street. The figure passed by her window before completely disappearing in the mist of the rain. Artemis got up and opened her window to see where it had gone. All she saw were cars and bicycles passing through the street. She was genuinely confused. There was no way a large white horse with a hooded rider could disappear quickly. She felt both confused and for the first time, scared. She quickly busied herself again with both her homework and the little pet project Jonathan proposed.

The men's dorm was quiet, save for some tenants who were either having drinking games or watching series on their laptops. Some would even go out partying, and stay out until the early morning hours. As a general consensus, most of the male students kept to themselves. Which made things feel odd for Milo Garnier, when he got an instant message from Jonathan Madden, asking if he could come over to his room.

Then again, of all the tenants in the dorm, it was only Jonathan who was extremely friendly with him. And he did have some treats from France. Perhaps Jonathan would like to try one. He began to look through his box and pulled out a large box of Bonne Maman Le Quatre-heures. He was sure Jonathan would like this. He would often munch on these every day back home. Especially during a rainy night like this, over coffee or cocoa.

He stood outside of Jonathan's dorm room carrying a small paper bag and a thermos. He knocked on the dorm room's door and waited. Jonathan opened the door and said. "I'm glad you could come. Come in."

Milo had never been inside another student's dorm room. In fact, he always wondered what it was like stepping into another student's room. He had always perceived Jonathan's dorm to have black linen, spray paint posters, anarchy symbols and all that. But instead, he was met with a clean and orderly looking room. There were posters of some heavy metal musicians on the wall, but there were no black or printed plaid beddings. There were no voodoo doll or occult shrines at all. It was an ordinary and simple room filled with books and a few hobby items.

"You have a very neat room, mon ami." Milo said, looking around.

"What, did you think I would have a lot of black, red and striped stuff?" Jonathan asked, somewhat reading the mind of the French student. Milo blinked, wondering how he somehow guess what was on his mind. Still, there was no guesswork needed. Jonathan probably had encountered a lot of people who assumed how his room looked like, simply by the way he dressed.

"Sort of." Milo admitted. " By the way, mon ami. I brought you some of the bonbons that Maman sent me." He opened the paper bag and pulled out the biscuits. "I also have a thermos of hot coffee. These treats are best enjoyed with coffee."

"Thank you, Milo." Jonathan said. "Why don't you sit there while I get the mugs and some plates." He pointed to his desk where there were two chairs. Milo sat by the chair and watched as Jonathan looked through his closet and things. He then noticed the laptop on his desk and the screen contents. He could see windows showing articles and content on Faustian contracts, Deals with devils, urban legend rituals and nursery rhymes.

Jonathan sat on the chair next to Milo and set a mug in front of him. Milo took out the thermos and poured out some hot coffee into both of the mugs. "So, you said you needed something of me?" Milo said,

"Yeah." Jonathan moved the laptop and showed Milo the laptop's multiple screens. "What do you know of Faustian contracts and Deals with the Devil?"

Chapter 4

If there was a rumor that would make it to the front page of a tabloid's newspaper, it would go something like this. 'College Girl Signs Million Dollar deal with Luxury brand.' Or 'College Girl to star in Local Adaptation of Hit Reality TV series.' Or even better. 'Famous Pop Star rumored to be in relationship with local College Girl.' Those kinds of headlines would really make for good sales and interesting reads. Even if they did sound quite farfetched.

Not in Claire's case. She had never been this lucky at all. Yes, she was a popular fixture in the campus' party scenes. But never to an extent that almost everything glamorous could happen to her. The last thing she remembered was attending a party in one of the frat houses in Greek row, before going out to a crossroad for something.

She can't seem to remember what she was doing there, other than she was there for a reason. All she did remember was a taxi driving up to her and asking her where she was headed. And when she got inside the taxi, she could see a glamorous looking ruby ring.

When she got up to her dorm room, she found Artemis studying as usual. She saw Artemis flinch a bit and cover her nose. "God, you smell like an open bar. How many bottles did you drink?"

"Not much." Claire said with a bit of a slur in her reply. "Just the usual....5 bottles." She walked to her side of the room and slumped into her bed.

"Are you alright?" Artemis asked. "You don't look so good."

"Yeah." She said. "Just a bit tired. I think I'll rest. But...I feel good. Like I feel...like a winner."

"Okay, that is weird." Artemis said as she wrote down the summary of her findings. Claire stretched a bit and pulled off the clothes from her person, before throwing them in her clothes bin. She took her towel and headed to the bathroom to shower. She undid her hairclip and saw the ruby ring on her finger. And ten, she suddenly remembered where she had gotten the ring.

The crossroads she had gone to after the party and the steps she had done. She remembered the sound of clip clopping hooves, and the appearance of a beautiful woman dressed entirely in white. She remembered how she spoke to the lady, and how the lady responded by giving her one of her rings before riding away.

She suddenly realized that she had done it. She had actually summoned the Lady on the Horse. Oh, why did it take so long for her to remember? Was this an after effect of meeting the Lady on the Horse?

Regardless, despite feeling inebriated, she felt like something good was going to happen, and decided not to take off the ring as she turned on the shower. After all, this was going to be her good luck charm.

She woke up the next morning with the fresh morning sun hitting her face. She reached for her phone, checked the time and gasped. If she didn't get up and get dressed quickly, she would be late for first period. Worse, it was going to be an exam! She rushed to the bathroom and took a quick shower. Next, she ran to the closet and began to pull out some clean clothes, when Artemis came into the room from her morning jog.

"Whoa, what's got you so worked up?" she asked as she watched Claire slip on her underthings.

"No time to talk." Claire replied. "Going to be late for first period."

"Oh, you didn't hear?" Artemis said. "First period has been cancelled for today."

What? Claire stopped combing her hair and looked at Artemis. "What did you say? First period is cancelled? We don't have the same class."

"No, but the department heads called all the teachers for some assembly." She replied. "Next class is gonna be after lunch. Which is good because I at least can jog before the weather changes."

First period was cancelled? Claire didn't know that. And all departments too, no less? That was a mighty strange and convenient coincidence. She looked at the ruby ring on her finger and wondered if this had anything to do with what she asked from the Lady on the Horse.

Well there was no point in hurrying now. She thought to herself, and at the very least she could take a proper quick bath and go to the gym with her friends. After all, she had a long time until next period and a lot could happen. She took her phone and began to message her friends for a quick meet up at the college gym. She then put on some exercise clothes, grabbed her water bottle and headed out to the gym.

She found her friends Annamarie, Jane and Yvonne waiting for her at the entrance of the college gym. "Hey girl, you look good for someone's who had five bottles of vodka and tequila." Yvonne said as they entered the gym. "It sure is a good thing first period class was cancelled."

"Yeah." Annamarie said. "What was the reason?"

"Something about some assembly." Yvonne said.

"Either way, that was a relief." Claire said as they signed their names in the gym logbook. "At least we'll avoid the surprise exam by Dr. Lewis."

"Aww, that means you won't get to see Jonathan Madden." Jane teased. Claire ignored that remark as the four girls headed towards the row of treadmills that stood side by side facing a large window. As they stepped on the treadmills, the girls began to chat as usual on topics they liked the most.

The latest gossip in the celebrity news. The hottest trends in, and dare we say it, social media influencers. The upcoming sales from their favorite clothing stores. And more importantly, the next frat party. Claire, however, didn't seem too interested in what they were talking about. Frankly speaking, her thoughts were more on what had happened the night before.

She could still remember seeing the large horse approach her as she stood in the center of the crossroad. She remembered seeing the lady in her head. Even if she couldn't recall her features.

"Hey girl" Yvonne said as they ran on the treadmills. "You okay there?"

"Yeah, why do you ask?" Claire said as she increased the inclination on her own machine.

"You're not talking about Jonathan Madden like you normally would." Jane said. "Don't tell me you asked him out again?"

"No, I didn't." She replied. "Not yet that is. I have a feeling that something good is going to happen."

"What makes you say that?" Annamarie asked in between exhales.

"Well, first period was cancelled, right?" Claire said. "I have a feeling that today is gonna be a good day. I just know it."

"Yeah, well I'll believe ya if it does happen." Jane said. After a couple of minutes on the treadmills, the girls went to the coffee stand across the gym for some coffee. As they sipped on their coffee, a barista walked over to their table. "Hello." The barista said. "We're having an instant prize contest. We have many prizes at stake including a spokesmodel contract."

"What, a spokesmodel contract?" Jane said. "That is something."

"Check under your cups." The barista said again.

The girls looked under the cups as instructed. "I won a designer tumbler." Yvonne said.

"I won a month's worth of coffee!" Annamarie said.

"I won a planner and bag set." Jane said.

"I-I-"They heard Claire stammer. Her friends looked at Claire as she stared at her cup. "I..."

"What is it, Claire?" Yvonne asked.

"I won the spokesmodel contract." She replied. The entire coffee kiosk was silent for a moment as they looked at Claire O Hara.

Let us assume for this very moment, that this is a statistical mathematics class. The basis of statistics operates on the fundamentality of ratios. There are almost 5 billion people in the State. And there are almost 100 coffee kiosks scattered all over. On average, the kiosk would serve 2000 people in one day. And when it came to prizes, there would only be at least four major prizes at stake. So, it stands to reason, that the probability of winning such a grand prize would be on a ratio of 1 to 1,000.

Those were very difficult odds. And for some, they'd like to increase the odds of winning by purchasing more. Who would have thought that in one purchase, Claire O Hara would win one of the coveted grand prizes?

"Oh my gosh." Annamarie said. "You won the contract?!"

"That is so fabulous!" Yvonne said.

"Congratulations." The barista said to Claire as he handed her an envelope. "Please check the contents of the envelope and here is our corporate building's address. I've already messaged the marketing department and they are dying to meet you." He then excused himself and went back to his post.

The girls were extremely excited and happy for their friend. They began to praise Claire for her winnings. "Wow, you were right about one thing. "Jane said. "You said something good was going to happen."

"Did you go to some fortune teller and ask about the future?" Annamarie said.

"No." Claire said with a confident air. "But I'm going to enjoy the day." She got up and told her friends that she was heading out to the corporate address. She then bid them goodbye and walked back to her dorm.

Upon entry, she saw Artemis looking over some clothes on her bed. "What are you doing?" She asked, observing Artemis's confused and slightly troubled face.

"Well, I'm trying to pick appropriate clothes for this afternoon." Artemis said. "And the fact that the forecast is going to be somewhat gloomy and wet, I'm considering something warm and long sleeved."

Claire suddenly remembered that today was the afternoon 'date' Artemis spoke of. She then plopped down on the bed and said. "Oh right, today is your afternoon date. And you still won't tell me who you're dating?"

"For the last time, it's not a date." Artemis said. "Besides, I'll say it again. What's it to you on who I'm seeing?"

"Well, I am your roommate and I cannot let my roommate go on a date looking like she's working at the library." Claire said.

"Gee, that's a comfort to know." She said in a slightly sarcastic tone. She wasn't one for vanity and looks, and she wasn't the type who would listen to people like Claire. Still, there was a slight hint that she had good intentions in her statement. She could see Claire scanning the clothes on the bed, studying them with great scrutiny, as though she were an expert in the delicate art of antiquities and carbon dating. Or at the very least, an expert in details.

"Did you have an outfit in mind?" Claire asked

"Well…" Artemis began. "I was going for this sweater and these pants." She pointed to an oversized sweater and paint splattered pants. Claire raised an eyebrow and asked. "And you said it's going to be a coffee date?"

"Again, not a date." Artemis repeated. "And yes, it's a coffee shop thing."

"Well, you can't go there wearing that." Claire said, getting up and rummaging through Artemis' side of the closet. "God, you don't even have anything sexy here."

"I don't have time or the need to have sexy clothes." Artemis folded her arms. "And I don't understand why you're 'helping 'me."

"I'm in a good mood." Claire said, studying shirt after shirt. "I got really lucky today and I'm in the mood to share my good fortune." She stopped at a blouse and smiled. "Oh, this is sexy." She pulled it out. It was a thin strapped blouse made out of white eyelet lace and cut in a corset-like shape. "Why don't you wear stuff like this?"

"Because I only wear that if I'm wearing a cardigan." She replied.

"Well, wear it as is." Claire said. "And also, these." She pulled out a pair of dark blue jeans. "This is like the perfect date outfit."

"For the last time, it's not a- "Artemis had somehow given up. She could see that Claire was in a good mood and even if it was just a spur of the moment thing, it was better than the usual snickering she would get from Claire.

"You know…" Claire continued in a matter of fact tone that Artemis was quick to notice. "You're really hot and pretty. Why don't you try that ritual?"

"What ritual?" she asked.

"Ever heard of that rhyme, 'Ride a Cock Horse'?" Claire said. "Well, there is a ritual that if you do it, success and wishes will all be realized."

"It sounds like one of those games you play during sleepovers like Bloody Mary or Charlie, Charlie." Artemis said. "Do you really believe it works?"

"You never know." Claire replied. "You should try it." After selecting the outfit for Artemis and laying it on her bed, she picked up her own towel and headed to the shower for a long, refreshing bath. After all, if she was going to sign the spokesmodel contract, she had to look both refreshed and energized. She got out and changed into clothes. Picking up her bag, she walked to the door.

"Well, I'm off." She told Artemis. "Have fun at your date." She giggled and left the room.

****

Claire hailed a cab and traveled towards the address written on the envelope. While in the cab, she opened the envelope and took a look at its contents. There was the modeling contract and several coupons for free gifts. She read the contract and was surprised to see how much she would be earning. The cab stopped at a tall building with large glass windows. Claire got off, walked inside and inquired for the head of marketing. The concierge directed her to a waiting lounge. Claire walked to the lounge and sat on one of the sofas. Sitting across from her was a man dressed in a suit. He was eyeing her from head to toe. He had a scrutinizing look, which, in a way, bothered her immensely. Then, he approached her and said. "Has anyone ever told you that you have a great physique?"

Claire looked at him and said. "Yeah, my fitness instructor said I really have toned abs. Wow, this makes the spokesmodel gig easy as pie."

"How would you like to have a modeling contract with Pandora Models?" he asked producing a calling card from his jacket.

Claire knew of Pandora Models; it was one of the country's most famous modeling agencies. She knew of the agency's former models. Most of them had transitioned from modeling to acting to even running their own modeling agencies. She couldn't believe her stroke of luck as the man handed her the card. He went on to say that if she had time, she could drop by the agency.

"I'm sure we won't need for a resume and photo samples." He said when she asked him. "In fact, I'm sure they'll even give you a contract."

Another modeling contract? She couldn't believe her luck. When she finally got to meet the marketing heads for the spokesmodel contract, they had surprised her with a bonus that was twice the amount of her own tuition. After signing the contract, she quickly left the building, carrying in her bag, the large amount of money just waiting to be spent. She looked at her watch. There was still time for her to go to Pandora Models before the next period.

She raised her hand and tried to hail a cab. As the car slowly approached her, Claire suddenly felt a strong gust of cold wind blow. She looked up to see the sky. It was still sunny and bright. She looked around and saw a strange mist forming in the distance. Why was there mist? She thought as he heard the cab stop in front of her. She opened the door and got inside and directed the cab driver to take her to Pandora Models. As the cab drove away, Claire looked over her shoulder and saw the strange mist still forming in the distance.

****

"I'm sorry, mon ami." Milo said, looking at Jonathan as he sat on the desk. "Deals with ze Devil? Mon dieu zat is a topic that my family and I avoid as much as possible."

"Oh?" Jonathan asked. "Why is that?"

"It is not obvious, but I am Catholic." Milo replied. "And we are quite religious in our understanding of evil both seen and unseen."

"I see." Jonathan said. "I'm sorry if I touched on a topic that makes you uncomfortable."

"Oh no, not at all." Milo poured another cup of coffee from his thermos. "Zat doesn't mean I can't 'elp you. So, what do you want to know?"

"Overall understanding." He replied. "You're a literature major. I'm sure there must be a root story in all this." Milo leaned back against the chair and thought about the question. Jonathan looked at Milo's expression. Perhaps he must have asked a rather difficult question. Jonathan thought.

"To be honest, mon ami." Milo began. "Zere are so many stories about deals with ze devil told throughout various cultures. I am sure you know about Faust, yes?"

"If I'm not mistaken, Faust was a doctor and alchemist who asked the devil, Mephistopheles, to grant him immense knowledge, power and the devil's service." He replied. "In return, Mephistopheles will serve Faust for a set number of years. Once the years end, he will claim Faust's soul as payment."

"Grim to zink about it no?" Milo said. "Faust gets what he wants, but when ze deadline approaches, he slowly begins to regret ze deal."

Jonathan tried to picture himself in the shoes of the man. What could have gone through his mind when he made that decision? Was he constantly ridiculed for his ideas? Was he constantly compared to someone of a more reputable standing? Did he want to satisfy his prideful urges to subject a powerful being to his beck and call? And what happened after he got his wish? He wondered if he felt satisfaction or greed.

"Does the story ever tell of what Faust felt?" he asked.

"Don't know, mon ami." Milo replied. "But his story isn't ze only one of ze nature. In France, zere is talk about zis orchestra leader named Philippe Musard who was popular with theaters. And zen zere's zat musician. Robert Johnson?"

"Yeah." Jonathan said. "Legend goes that he was walking to a crossroad one gloomy night and came in contact with a stranger dressed nicely. The stranger turned out to be the devil, who offered him the uncanny mastery of the guitar and the ability to play it." He stopped for a moment. There was something vaguely familiar with that story.

"Does zis 'ave anything to do with zat nouveau ritual game?" Milo asked. "Zat whole Lady on ze 'orse?"

"Not really, no." Jonathan replied. "But...truth be told, I keep hearing it around campus. Most of the girls think it's real. Even Artemis' roommate thinks it's real...."

Here, Milo Garnier gave Jonathan a sly smirk and said. "Artemis? Ees Zat ze girl you were seeing earlier?"

Jonathan stammered, not expecting to say her name out. He had tried his best to keep things to himself, especially when it came to things that could be misinterpreted by others. Still, there was no helping it; he had said her name himself. Better to roll with the punches, they say. "Yeah, Artemis Rosi." He said. "She's a History major..."

"Wait a minute." Milo said as though Jonathan had something familiar. "Rosi? As in George Rosi?"

"Who's George Rosi?" He asked.

Milo gasped as he replied. "George Rosi is ze foremost expert on historical literature and modern-day adaptations. He's written books and articles on Historical adaptations in literature."

Possible relative? A dad maybe? Jonathan thought. That would make sense with her taking up History. Maybe she wants to help him in his research. That was the most probable reason. Milo went on. "Did you ask if she was related to George Rosi? If so, think she can get me an autograph?"

"Can we get back to the subject?" Jonathan said. "In a way, it does have something to do with that ritual. But I personally don't think it's real."

"If you zink eet's not real, zen why are you somewhat invested with eet?" he asked.

That is a very good question. He thought. If he didn't think it was real, then why was he interested in it? "I can tell you zis." Milo added. "Evil and sin are around us. Both seen and unseen. And no matter 'ow desperate we are for success, fame and fortune, we must not be tempted. For it is a choice zat we will regret and damn our souls to Hell."

Jonathan took into consideration the last statement he made. He didn't want to tell Milo what he had seen earlier. After all, it could have been his overactive mind creating the image of the silhouette in the curtain. But then again, why that particular silhouette. Either way, he did get some insight from Milo's stories. But perhaps there was more. And the library might have the answer he needed.

The next day, Jonathan walked towards the library to look at some books on certain topics for his homework. There was something about the library that appealed greatly to Jonathan. The university's library was a large building that was reminiscent of the old Streamline Moderne style that was famous in the early 40s. The interior also spoke of the same style, with massive shelves stacked with books, portraits of famous figures and landscape sceneries, comfortable sofas and tables and chairs occupied by students reading and studying. Jonathan walked to the computerized catalogs and began to type into the search engines.

"Mr. Madden." Jonathan heard the voice of Dr. Lewis. He turned to see Dr. Lewis walking towards him. "Doing homework?" he asked.

"Uh, something like that." Jonathan said. Dr. Lewis looked at the screen and noticed the titles. "Hmm...Folklore and Folktales of America. Are you interested in understanding what made folklore commonplace?" Dr. Lewis asked.

"Something like that, Dr. Lewis." He replied. "I was reading a chapter in one of my textbooks, and I came across several anecdotes on supernatural dealings in society."

"Ah, I know that one." Dr. Lewis said. "So, you want to know why most societies will attribute sudden success to dealings with the devil, right?"

"Yeah." Jonathan said.

"Well, good luck in your studies." Dr. Lewis said. "Which reminds me, have you thought about my internship yet? I'm still looking for applicants, and so far, I only have two. I could really use an additional pair of hands."

"Uh, yeah." He replied. "I haven't gotten round to emailing my resume yet. What with all the subjects and homework and stuff."

"I see." Dr. Lewis said. He then excused himself and walked to the librarian's desk to check out some books. Jonathan, having gotten the book numbers and location, hurriedly walked to the bookcases to look for the books. As he scanned through the titles on the book spines, he could hear a group of boys whispering to one another a few shelves away.

"...have you ever kissed her?" one asked.

"...better. I danced with her." Another one replied.

"Claire O'Hara is such a hottie." Another boy said. "And I heard she just signed two modeling contracts."

"That is major hottie points right there." The first boy said.

Claire O'Hara? Wasn't that the name of the girl who talked about the Lady on the Horse ritual with her friends during Dr. Lewis's class? Jonathan thought, then went on with his book search as he listened in.

"I heard she's started her modeling this morning." A boy said. "Wonder what it would be like to date a model?"

Jonathan heard the boys slowly walk away. 'Finally, some peace and quiet.' He thought. He found one out of three books that he was looking for. He could see just how old and frayed the book covers were. He looked at the title. *Folktales and Legends*. The pages were also slightly torn and yellow in age; perhaps others had borrowed this book more often than not.

He began reaching for the next book, when he suddenly heard a strange voice singing an all too familiar rhyme. "*Ride a cock horse to Banbury cross. To see a fine lady upon a white horse...Rings on her fingers and bells on her toes. And she shall have music...wherever she goes...*"

He looked through the space in between the book shelves for the source of the singing voice. But he couldn't see anything or anyone. The voice slowly began to grow louder; as if someone were approaching him. Suddenly, he could hear the sound of bells coming from behind. He turned around and saw nothing. Slowly, he let out a cold breath of air as the singing grew louder and louder.

And then he saw it, out of the corner of his eye, a strange, white shape standing behind one of the bookcases a few meters away. He looked to the direction of the shape and squinted for a bit. The shape looked strangely familiar. Then he knew what it was.

It was the shape of the woman in white he saw through the shower curtains. He had begun walking towards the woman when he suddenly felt light headed. He slowly leaned against a bookcase as he tried to get his bearings back. He felt like something or someone was weighing him down, and he just couldn't figure out how. He slowly looked up and saw that his vision was getting blurry. And yet he could still see the shape of the woman, who, to his immediate surprise, was walking towards him.

"Who are you?" he asked groggily, still leaning against a bookcase. The woman was slowly approaching him, and at that moment, the song had grown louder to the point that it was the only thing he could hear.

"Ride a cock horse to Banbury cross. To see a fine lady upon a white horse...Rings on her fingers and bells on her toes. And she shall have music...wherever she goes..."

He looked at the woman and could see what he assumed was her face. But it was a face that sent chills up his spine. Before he could register the features, Jonathan slowly dropped to his knees and collapsed to the floor.

****

He could hear frantic voices around him as a hand gently patted his cheek. A strong, slightly chemical scent permeated under his nose, causing him to stir awake. He slowly opened his eyes and saw the librarian and the university nurse surrounding him; a small bottle of smelling salts in the nurse's hand.

"Thank goodness he's come to." The librarian said. "Are you alright, young man?"

"Yeah, I'm alright." Jonathan said as he slowly got up. "What happened?"

"You must have passed out." The nurse replied. "Have you been eating or sleeping properly? Perhaps you need to rest more?"

"I'm fine, don't worry." He replied. "Listen. Have any of you seen a woman dressed in white?"

The librarian and the nurse looked at one another in a confused manner. "I'm sorry, dear, but what do you mean dressed in white?"

"Umm, okay forget that." Jonathan said. "Was anyone ringing bells or singing an old nursery rhyme?"

"Are you sure you're alright?" the librarian asked. "Perhaps you do need to rest in the clinic."

"No, I'm alright, I promise." He said. Does it mean they didn't see the woman and hear the rhyme? He thought. If so, what was going on? He assured the nurse and the librarian that he was alright. Then, he checked out the books he wanted and immediately left the library.

This was the second time he had seen the strange woman, and he was beginning to think that there was something strange happening at the university. Either way, he was sure it had something to do with the Lady on the Horse. He quickly pulled his phone out and dialed a number. "Come on, pick up...Artemis...Hi, it's Jonathan. .... listen, um...can I see you today? It's really important.... really? Ok cool, so...the campus coffee shop? Ok, see you." He pocketed his phone and hurried over to the coffee shop.

Chapter 5

"Look this way, darling!" There was a bright flash of light as Claire was surrounded with men carrying cameras, and makeup artists bustling around with makeup cases. She had never been in a professional photoshoot, let alone wear such beautiful and glamorous looking clothes. She had never been waited on hand and foot, and more importantly, she had never had people shower her with compliment upon compliment.

"You're a natural!" the photographer said. "Now, give me a little fun face."

Claire flipped her hair and gave the photographer what he wanted. When they checked the photo reels, it was clear to everyone that a dilemma had presented itself. All of her photos were beautifully taken and they had to decide which one they would use. As the photographers worried over the rather difficult decision, Claire walked to the holding area and had her hair redone.

"Wow, you did great." One of the models sitting nearby said. "This is your first shoot, right?"

"For a first timer, you're pretty good." Another model said.

'For a first timer? No, I'm a natural.' Claire thought as the hair stylist began to comb her hair. I've always been a natural when it came to the camera. And I keep my body in shape. So, if one would look at it, those clothes were made for me. She then saw several male celebrities who had come for the shoot. She would see how handsome and good looking they were. She even recognized some of them from magazines and TV shows.

She saw one of them approach her. She knew who he was; she had seen him in one of her favorite TV series. Randy Fairbanks. He was a good-looking man with brown and blonde hair, and very handsome green eyes. He had a firm chest and a sexy smile that could make just about anyone melt. "Hello..." he said with a handsome tone. "I'm Randy. You really look great in those shots."

"Gee, thanks." Claire said.

"Is this your first time?" he asked.

"Yes."

"Well, you're a natural." 'Oh my gosh.' She thought to herself. He complimented her and said she was a natural. "Say, I was wondering, would you be interested in going out to dinner with me tomorrow?"

"Oh, I'd like that." Claire said.

"So, tomorrow say...6pm at the Chez Panisse?" he asked, pulling out his phone and getting her number. Claire could not believe what was happening. Here was one of the most famous celebrities asking her out to dinner at one of the city's most fabulous and luxurious restaurants. As he walked to the shoot, the other models began to crowd around Claire, and started to compliment her on her upcoming date and incredible circumstance.

"Oh my gosh!" the first model began. "You're going on an actual date with Randy Fairbanks."

"I heard he's loaded in his own right." another model said.

"Well, that's expected of a guy who's related to Douglas Fairbanks." Another model added. "That is a sure-fire way to become famous."

"You are so lucky!"

Lucky? She thought to herself as she looked at the ruby ring on her finger. 'It's not luck. It's the wish she gave me.' She thought. As soon as the shoot was over, she packed her things into her bag and walked out of the studio. She stood by the roadside and was trying to hail a cab, when a bright, red sports car drove up towards her. The driver lowered his window to reveal the handsome features of Randy at the wheel.

"Hi again." He said. "What are you doing out here?"

"Waiting for a cab." She replied. "I still go to college and I have to get back in time for my next class."

"I can drive you." Randy said as he opened the passenger seat door. "Come on in."

"Really, you don't mind?" She asked.

"Well, it looks like it's about to rain." He replied. "Besides, cabs are hard to find at this hour." True to his word, the sky slowly grew dark and gloomy, and little droplets of rain began to fall. "Come on in or you'll catch a cold."

Claire, seeing no cabs coming in, quickly got inside Randy's red sports car. As she fastened her seatbelt, Randy held out a dry face towel to her. "Here, you can use this." He said. Claire wiped her face dry and leaned back against the car seat, as Randy drove along the now rain-soaked streets.

If you could imagine what it was like to be sitting in the car of a famous celebrity, who not only offered you a ride, but also helped you out of the pouring rain, you'd probably feel like you were floating on the clouds. Or maybe you'd think this would be a euphoric dream you never want to wake up from. But Claire had a different feeling in all this. It was a feeling of indulgence; that everything was due her. So, it was only natural that someone as famous and good looking as Randy Fairbanks would drive her to college.

"You know," Randy started. "You are really...really...pretty." And he began to compliment and talk to her about how she seemed to be an overnight sensation, and how things were looking brighter for her. They reached a stop light and continued their chat. Claire leaned back against the car seat and listened to the sound of the rain, the car radio and...the sound of clip clopping hooves.

She suddenly sat upright and looked through the densely covered window and looked out into the streets. What was that strange sound she just heard? Hooves? Were there horses out?

"Are you alright?" Randy asked, noticing how she suddenly looked quite scared. "Did you just think of something?"

"Did you hear that strange sound?" she asked.

"What strange sound?" he asked

"It sounded like.... hooves." Claire looked out the window. "Like hooves...of a horse."

"I'm sorry. I didn't hear anything." Randy said.

Claire looked again through the window and when she was sure there was nothing, she settled back into the seat and chuckled nervously. "Maybe it was all those flashing lights that's making me out of sorts."

"Well, that happens most of the time." Randy said. "You'll get used to it. But you have to rest once in a while." The red light turned green and they slowly resumed the drive. Claire let out a sigh of relief as Randy smiled at her and drove. After all, life was starting to get better for her. There was no way a strange sound would end it completely.

****

All the girls gathered around to crane their necks out of their dorm room windows, to get a better look outside; some even had their phones out. A shiny, red sports car had driven up to the front of the girl's dormitory. The driver had climbed out of the car, and to the tenants' excited surprise, it was none other than famous actor and model, Randy Fairbanks. All the girls began to giggle and mutter among themselves. Why was a celebrity parked outside a college dorm? They watched as Randy walked to the other side of the car and opened the passenger side door. The girls couldn't believe who it was that got out of the car; it was Claire O' Hara!

Immediately, they began to talk once more as they saw Randy Fairbank kiss Claire on the cheek and bid her farewell. As the car drove away, Claire walked to the main door and got inside. She came face to face with her three friends Yvonne, Annamarie and Jane. Behind them were the other residents of the dorm. They quickly crowded around Claire and began to ask her.

"Oh my God, was that Randy Fairbank?" Yvonne asked.

"Did you come from your photoshoot?" Jane added. "Was he at the photoshoot?"

"Speaking of which, you look good!" Yvonne said. "Are those new clothes from the photoshoot?" She was alluding to the new clothes and things Claire was wearing. For a college student, the notion of wearing luxurious brands was a dream. And Claire was no exception to having such a dream. Particularly if the dream was a reality. She wore a beautiful Versace blouse that looked as if it had been tailored specifically for her, a pair of the famous red sole Louboutin shoes, a Swarovski jeweled necklace and finally, a beautiful Prada purse.

"Yes." Claire replied. "They're tokens from the designers for my beautiful shots. I dare say I'll make them famous with my looks." There was a sense of pomp and pride in her tone. It was natural, of course. Who wouldn't feel the satisfying sense of validation and admiration from people you once aspired to be and more? "And tomorrow, I'm having dinner with Randy Fairbanks at the Chez Panisse restaurant." She added.

There were 'oohs' and 'aahs' and 'oh my god's' coming from her friends and the girls surrounding her. A college student dating a famous celebrity? That was something of a dream come true for most girls.

"Oh my God!" One of the girls began. "You are the luckiest girl in the world!"

"He's totally into you!" Annamarie said. Yvonne leaned in and whispered into Claire's ear. "Don't you think that's a lot better than having Alex Madden's little brother ignore you? You did better."

'I did do better.' Claire thought to herself as she basked in the compliments from the girls. So what if I can't date Alex Madden's little brother? I'm already a model! A soon to be discovered talent. And I'm having dinner with the most gorgeous and devilishly handsome Randy Fairbanks. She excused herself and went up the stairs to her room.

She walked into her room and saw her roommate, Artemis wrapping her wet hair with a towel and sitting by her desk in a white and blue kimono. "So, did you go on another date?" she asked.

Artemis looked up and said. "Oh, you're back. Sorry, I had other things to worry about. Plus, it's raining. And it's not a date."

"Well, let's wait for it." Claire said as she tossed her bag on top of her bed. "Mark my words, he's bound to ask you out again. Now seriously…" She sat on her chair and looked at Artemis." Are you ever gonna tell me who the guy is?"

"No." Artemis said. "Because it's none of your business."

"Are you at least going to have like…a spa date?" She asked, eyeing Artemis from head to toe.

"No, because it's not necessary and it's a bit expensive."

"I'll hook you up." Claire pulled out her phone. "Seriously, you are like that ugly duckling girl in that 90's movie. The one with Freddie Prinze?" She began to dial a number and started to speak on the phone. After what seemed like a few minutes, she hung up on the phone. "Okay, you're all set. I've booked you a spa at the Bella du Amor Spa. Don't worry about the cost, okay?"

"You don't really have to." Artemis said.

"You're my pet project." She exclaimed. "And besides, I can't possibly be known to have a roommate who looks like she's…. a commoner."

"Wow, thanks for that then." Artemis raised an eyebrow, slightly unhinged with that statement. But as always, Claire was the type who couldn't see reason. Even if she did say a few unpleasant things. Then again, Claire could give her insight on things. After all, the odds of having your luck turn for the better were astronomically improbable. She knew that for a fact.

"But..." Claire would continue. "Makeovers aren't the only thing that can make your life better. You gotta work for it."

That sort of sounds hypocritical of her, she thought. Considering that a few days ago, she was just like everybody else, save for the need to party and would never pick up a textbook or two. So, it was quite odd indeed for someone like Claire to preach about working for something.

"Now, that doesn't mean you don't need a little help." Claire said. "You should try everything possible."

"Even...I don't know...wishing games?" Artemis asked.

Claire looked at Artemis as though she had said something right. She then replied. "Well, yeah, that too. I mean, I have tried a lot of those games and wouldn't you know it, my luck has turned out the best." She got up and took off her clothes and put on her sleeping clothes. "Are you going to be up all night?" she asked.

"Not really, I'm just gonna read a few more chapters. Then I'll sleep." Artemis replied. "Why?"

"Well, I'll need to sleep early. I've had a very awesome day and I intend to have another awesome day tomorrow." Claire got into bed, placed an eye mask over her eyes and went to sleep. Today was a great day, she thought. And tomorrow will be even greater. She yawned and slowly drifted off to sleep.

****

Cameras were flashing all over, as Claire walked down the luxurious felted red carpet towards a large building. Walking alongside her with his arm looped around her right arm was Randy Fairbanks. In the other was another handsome looking celebrity. She beamed with happiness and delight as photographers took her photo and reporters interviewed her along the way.

The Overnight Wonder, they would soon call her. And tonight was the premiere of her breakout movie role. And she even looked the part herself. She was dressed in a beautiful Balenciaga gown and had a fur shawl wrapped around her arms. She had sparkling Bulgari jewels, and her make up complimented the entire look.

A reporter walked up to her and began to interview her. "Claire, tell us. How do you feel tonight?"

'What a question.' She thought as she looked at the glittering stars at night and replied. "I feel magical. This is a dream come true."

"Tell us what's going on in your mind." The reporter said, holding out the microphone to her. Claire leaned in and answered. "I'm just so happy. Everything is perfect. Like nothing can spoil it."

"What is your secret?"

"Oh, hard work." She enumerated. "Dedication. Perseverance..."

"Making decisions?" The reporter added ominously. "Making a pact?" Claire blinked at the reporter's statement. She looked up to the reporter to see that the reporter was gone. She then looked to her sides, both Randy Fairbanks and the other man were gone!

The photographers had disappeared and the beautiful building with the bright lights had crumbled down, until it was nothing more than an ugly pile of rubble. The luxurious red carpet was now frayed and tattered, as though it had been decades since it saw its splendor. Claire suddenly found herself in what looked like the ruins of a once beautiful theater. There was an abundance of over growth and vines, and an overbearing sense of isolation and horror.

Claire couldn't comprehend what was happening. How did she end up in this place? And where was everyone? She then heard a strange, girlish voice singing.

"Ride a cock horse to Banbury cross. To see a fine lady upon a white horse...Rings on her fingers and bells on her toes.

And she shall have music...wherever she goes..."

That rhyme. She thought. The rhyme that her parents used to sing to her when she was a little girl. The rhyme that, for some reason, was ominous and foreboding. She heard the voice constantly echo all over the area. Then she heard the sound of twinkling bells and raspy, horse-like grunts. She looked around and saw a strange mist slowly come forward. She was compelled to walk away from the rubble.

As she did so, she heard the sound of hooves coming towards her. Slowly, they creeped at a rather calming pace. But there was something in Claire's fiber that made her want to walk faster. After all, the reporter's question and the sudden change in the place were things that generally frightened her. She walked faster, lifting the bits of her skirt and taking care not to stumble. The hooves started to move fast as well, almost as if it were galloping. Claire quickly picked up the pace and began to run. And as she started to run, along came a loud and menacing neigh as she looked over her shoulder.

She would see a ghastly looking sight; a large, white, skeletal horse with menacing red eyes charging towards her. On the back was a hooded figure dressed in white flowing robes, and charging the horse to gallop faster. Claire stumbled as she ran and quickly took off her heels and started to sprint. She ran as fast as she could, her heart was racing as ever. She looked over her shoulder once more and her eyes widened with fear.

The horse and the hooded figure were now approaching her at an uncanny speed. She tried to look for a place to hide, but there was nothing in the barren grounds. Her feet were now covered with freshly open blisters and limp from strain. She then collapsed to the ground and began to crawl as fast as she could. The horse was now edging closer and closer to her, and she could see the hooded figure reach out to her with long skeletal hands.

Claire could now see a face under the folds of the hood. She screamed as she came face to face with a skeletal visage with dark, hollowed eyes, and a wide, toothy grin that stretched from ear to ear. She screamed even more as the skeletal face opened its mouth and let out a piercing shrill that made her ears bleed. She cried out in panic and closed her eyes as she heard her name being called. "Claire...Claire...Claire!"

"Claire! Claire! Wake up! Artemis said as she shook the frantic and crying Claire in her bed. "Wake up! Wake up!"

Claire opened her eyes and sat up in a jolt. 'That was all a dream?' She thought as she surveyed her surroundings. She was back in the dorm room. "Wha-what happened?" she groggily asked.

"Judging from the fact that you were thrashing about in your sleep and screaming so loud, I'd say you were having a nightmare." Artemis said. "That must have been a very nasty one at that."

"I was having a nightmare?" Claire repeated.

"Yeah. You were thrashing around in your bed and you were screaming and- "She stopped midsentence and looked closer. "Looks like your ear is bleeding." She took a tissue paper and gently dabbed it over Claire's ear. Claire would see there was indeed a small trail of blood on the tissue.

"My ear was bleeding?" Claire asked, thinking about the nightmare she had, and the unearthly scream that the hooded figure emitted. Artemis offered to take Claire to the clinic.

"It's not too far off and- "

"I'm fine, thank you." Claire interrupted briskly. "And you don't have to worry about me. I'm perfectly ok."

"But, your ear…"

"My ears are fine and I can hear perfectly." Claire said, then laid herself back to bed. "Thank you for your concern, but I need to sleep." And that she did. She went back to sleep.

Artemis just looked on at her. There was no way she was alright. In fact, if she were to pry even further, there was something in her tone of voice and her eyes that said otherwise. They spoke of fear and unknowing. They spoke of something that not even Claire could comprehend.

****

The next morning found Artemis asleep on the desk. Slowly, she stirred and stretched out her arms. She checked her phone and her schedule. She looked over her shoulder and saw that her roommate had already gone out for her class. She took a nice hot shower, changed into clean clothes, grabbed her bag and jacket and headed out of her dorm.

There was something about mornings after evening showers that were calming and refreshing for Artemis. She loved how the cool breeze blew around her and how the fallen leaves would rustle about. She loved the feel of her shoes stepping on the damp cobblestone path of the campus grounds. And best of all, she loved the smell of steaming hot coffee and freshly baked pastries in the air. She heard her stomach grumbling; she needed some breakfast.

She walked over to her favorite coffee stand and greeted the baristas. "Hey, Steve." She said. "Can I get a tall hot mocha and a large breakfast pastry to go, please?"

"Coming right up, Artemis." He replied as he went about preparing her order. As soon as she got her breakfast, she walked towards a bench and sat down. She took in the scent of the hot, buttery crust and the fragrant smell of mocha coffee, then took a bite out of the crust and sipped her coffee. 'Delicious', she thought to herself.

As she munched away, she couldn't help but think about what happened the night before. On a normal night, when Claire would return to the dorm room, she would be too exhausted from all that partying, that she would immediately go to sleep and have one of those uninterrupted, deep sleeps. Or if ever she would sleep, she wouldn't have fits from nightmares. But last night's fit was different. It was almost a frightening moment that neither Claire nor Artemis would want to relive again. The question was, what kind of nightmare would cause such a reaction?

"Did you hear?" Artemis would hear a couple of students behind her as they gossiped. "The student, Claire O'Hara, is seeing that famous model, Randy Fairbanks?"

"No way! Are you for real?"

"Positive! I heard it from my cousin who sent me the photo. He dropped her off at her dorm."

"I heard that too."

'She seems to be getting popular', she thought, slowly finishing her coffee and pastry. 'Then again, she's been wanting to be popular for some time now'. She got up and walked to the main building for her first morning class. First class of the day was English. She sat down in her usual seat and took out her notebook. She watched as the other students filed in, two of which she recognized as Claire's friends, Jane and Yvonne.

The teacher, Mr. Brewster, walked in carrying his satchel and greeted the class. "Today's lesson is all about the Ghosts in Literature." He said. "Now, who here can tell me about famous ghosts in literature?"

"Casper the Friendly Ghost." One male student said, and the entire classroom burst out laughing.

"Very funny, Mr. Samuels. But that's good." Mr. Brewster replied. "What else?"

"The Ghosts of Christmas Past, Present and Future." Jane said.

"Well done. Anymore?" Mr. Brewster asked. One by one, the students began to enumerate the ghosts they could think of.

"Hamlet's father."

"The Canterville Ghost."

"The kid from the Lovely bones."

"Patrick Swayze." Again, another burst of laughter erupted from the students. Mr. Brewster noticed Artemis staring at the window and asked. "Ms. Rosi, perhaps you know some ghosts from literature?"

Artemis turned to face him and said. "The Dullahan?"

The class looked confused; what was she talking about? What story did that come from? Mr. Brewster then said. "The Dullahan? Do continue..."

"He's basically what the Headless Horseman is based off of." She replied. "He's a spectral headless rider on a skeletal horse, with a whip made out of the spine of a human. He's basically the herald of death. If you see him, then that means you'll die."

The whole class was silent. Then, Mr. Brewster broke the silence. "That is a very interesting example. Which brings me to the big question. Why are people terrified and fascinated with ghosts?"

"Because they are dead and want to tell us something?" a student said.

"Exactly." Mr. Brewster said. "Simply put, ghosts, spirits, spectral beings are all harbingers. Messengers. Take Ms. Rosi's Dullahan for example. A spectral headless horse rider that brings about the death of an unfortunate soul. Or perhaps the Ghosts of Christmas Past, Present and Future, telling Scrooge what his fate would be, if he would not change for the better. They are more than just spirits of the departed. They are also a warning."

"A warning?" Yvonne asked.

"Yes." Mr. Brewster said. "That there are some things in this world that should never be challenged."

"So, does the Lady on the Horse count?" another student asked.

'I was wondering when someone would ask that.' Artemis thought. She could see the look in Mr. Brewster's eyes. The same skeptical and analytical look most educators had. "Ah, the quintessential Bloody Mary type." He replied. "I know the story. And it is a very saturated tale."

"There are people who say the story is true." One student added.

"And they will say it happened to a friend of a friend of a friend." Mr. Brewster added. "That is how stories evolve. When a simple story is told with added elements. One would even say, they create their own harbingers and messengers."

"But most stories have truths, right?" said another student.

"Oh yes. Most stories will definitely have a truth behind their fantastic premise." He replied. "The question now is, where is the fine line between fact and fiction." He went on to lecture how most authors would derive their stories from historical accounts. Which prompted Artemis to think of the question; was there a historical account to the story of the Lady on the Horse?

As soon as her last class for the day was over, she made her way to the campus café to meet up with Jonathan. She recalled the urgency in his tone when he called her for a meet up, and wondered if something happened or if he had found something. She entered the coffee shop and found him sitting in the dark corner of the room. She walked up and sat across him. "What was so urgent that you wanted to see me?" she asked.

"You will never guess what just happened." He said. "I saw something strange in the library."

"What do you mean?" she asked.

"I was researching about something a friend said." He began. "By the way, are you related to George Rosi?"

"He's my uncle. Why do you ask and why do you know about him?"

"Ah, my dorm neighbor, Milo." Jonathan said as the barista approached them and served them coffee. "Apparently, he idolizes your uncle very much and wants to get an autograph."

"Well." Artemis took a cup of coffee from the table. "If he wants, he could visit Uncle George in the office. Anyway, you were saying...."

"Right." Jonathan said. "Well, actually I had been thinking about the whole ritual itself. If I were to analyze the overall context, it's like making a deal with the devil."

"It's like a Faustian contract." Artemis said.

"Right and I asked my friend what he knew about it. He said that if one were to look at it, the person gets what he wants, but he slowly begins to regret it when the deadline for his payment comes up."

"Payment being his soul..."

Jonathan took a swig of coffee and let out a deep sigh. "So, I went to the library right after class today and tried to do some reading on the subject matter. I was looking through the bookshelves when I saw this ....hooded figure in white."

"A hooded figure in white?" Artemis repeated. Jonathan nodded and continued. "It was the second time I saw this figure, to be honest. But when I saw it, I felt terrified and fainted. But before all that, I kept hearing a strange voice singing that nursery rhyme."

He then leaned back against the chair as he studied Artemis's face. He waited for her to react strangely. But surprisingly, she was calm. She then asked. "So, you fainted in the library? Are you alright?"

"I am now." He replied. "In any case, I was genuinely spooked out. I never thought I'd see something like that."

"You and me both." Artemis said, setting her coffee cup down on the table. "Two nights ago, after you dropped me at my dorm, I went to my room to study. While I was studying, I saw a strange thing outside my window across the street."

"What did you see?" he asked

"Well, I'm not exactly sure." She replied. "But I swear it was a woman dressed in a white and gold robe on a large white horse. I thought it was weird at first. Like it was something I imagined. Until your story that is." She drummed her fingers together and added. "My roommate's still talking about how she's been lucky lately."

"Maybe she has."

Artemis raised an eyebrow at Jonathan, and gave a small snarky smirk. "My roommate is the kind of girl who would rather shop and party than pick up a book and study. And she talks about hard work and perseverance for her luck? No way."

Jonathan laughed, making Artemis blush a bit. Then he asked. "So, what did you find on your end? Any idea on where this story came from?"

"Historically? It's so vague." She replied. "But there is one thing I learned though. Spectral beings on horses tend to be harbingers or messengers of unfortunate news or fates. We could start with that."

'We could start with that.' Jonathan repeated as they continued to talk. They spent the next few minutes talking about what they discovered, while sipping more coffee. Finally, Artemis said. "Jonathan, I think.... I think my roommate tried the game."

"You think so?" he asked.

"It sounds silly to think, I know." She admitted. "But it seems to be the reason why she's so...euphoric with herself every day. But..." She looked down for a bit, moving the cup around in a circle. "It would explain why she had a nightmare and why she seems to be a bit on edge every now and then."

"A bit on edge?" he repeated.

"It's not obvious." She replied. "But you can see it in her eyes. She's afraid of something. And it's something she..."

"Regrets?" he finished.

She nodded. Jonathan settled back into his chair and thought about what Milo Garnier had once said. "There are evils both seen and unseen." And no matter how tempting the offer was, once a choice was made, there was no turning back. If her roommate did play the game and make the deal, what exactly was the price she chose to pay? And was she regretting it immensely?

Chapter 6

It was around 5 in the afternoon when Jonathan and Artemis finished their coffee and decided to leave the café together. It was a calm afternoon and the two friends decided it would be nice to walk together. As they walked along the stone pavements, Jonathan would glance at Artemis now and then. He felt a sense of happiness as though he were talking to an old friend.

He felt his heart beat at a rather strange yet passionate pace. He had never felt this kind of feeling before. In fact, he could remember the one time he felt this. It was when he first met a girl who often visited the house when he was younger. She was very pretty with brown hair and green eyes. She was sweet and kind. As a boy of maybe 13 or 15, Jonathan didn't know the difference between liking a girl and falling in love with one. He was deeply engrossed in books, music and gaming. But the very sight of the girl made his heart flutter. And when he confessed how he felt about her, the girl simply giggled and told him that he was just a boy and she was fairly attracted to his older brother.

Simply put, at that age, Jonathan had felt his first heart break. And when his brother Alex found him in a state of utter sorrow, he did what any older brother would do. He comforted the younger Madden, and that was when Jonathan decided that he would not be defined or be bothered by his brother. More importantly, the idea of having a girlfriend was something he was not too keen on, unless he would be willing to risk another broken heart.

But there was something different about Artemis. With her, he felt like that little 15 year old boy again, who was feeling all things both good and uncanny. Why was it that when he spoke to her, he felt like there were no other sounds apart from her own voice? Why was it that when he looked at her, everything around her would melt away to a beautiful black and white noir film where she would be dressed in a tailored suit and hat? Why was it that when she looked at him, he felt like he would want to be with her and only her?

"Jonathan?" Artemis' voice broke through his thoughts. He looked at her and replied. "Yes?"

"Are you alright with this?" she asked. "I mean, I have heard about your brother and how the girls would go after you." She gave a little giggle. "I wonder what would happen if they would see us right now?"

"Should that matter?" he quickly replied. "We are just friends..."

"I guess that is so..." she said. "We are friends.... Good friends." There was a slight strain in her voice as if she were content with that.

Why did I say that? He asked himself. Friends? Just friends? He looked at Artemis who gave him a friendly smile as they walked on further. They were approaching the main building, when they suddenly came face to face with none other than the most talked about student, Claire O' Hara. The two of them could see that she was dressed in a luxurious velvet looking dress, with a fur jacket and expensive looking sandals. She looked like she was going to a fancy party.

"Oh hello, Artemis." Claire said "Oh, you're acquainted with Jonathan Madden? That's nice. Are you in a class with him?"

"Hello Claire." Artemis said. "We became acquainted after he bumped into me by accident."

"I see..." Claire was looking at Jonathan from head to toe with the same admiration she had for him when she first realized who he was. "Oh, now I see...he's the one who asked you out, isn't he?" Jonathan could see how Claire was turning slightly red with embarrassment.

"So you're her roommate." He asked, not liking how she had inadvertently made Artemis a bit uncomfortable

"Ah she talks about me, I see." Claire said. "What does she say about me? Did she tell you that I was the one who picked out her outfit for your date night?"

"She did." Jonathan replied, taking care to use a more neutral tone with Claire.

"Well, we're on our way back to our dorms and we were just talking about this upcoming exhibit at the museum." Artemis said. "It's this very interesting exhibit on historical inspiration for famous writers. Maybe you'd like to go?"

"Thanks, but no thanks." Claire said in a haughty and condescending tone. "I'm heading to a dinner with Randy Fairbanks today." 'That would explain the fine-looking dress and fur coat.' Jonathan thought. She looked at him and added. "I'll say this about you, though. You're completely different from your brother."

They heard the sound of a car horn by the main gate. Claire turned around to see a red sports car. "Well, if you will excuse me, my date is here. Have a good evening, you two." She said, slightly dropping her tone further down as she walked towards the main gate and got into the car.

As soon as the car drove away, Jonathan looked at Artemis and quickly said. "Your roommate is full of herself."

"I know." She sighed.

"Are you alright?" he asked.

"Shouldn't I be asking you that?" Artemis looked at him and they both chuckled. "But seriously, don't worry about me. I'm sort of used to that."

"Well, you shouldn't." Jonathan said. "And she should mind her own business." Then, it dawned on him. "Wait, if she played that ritual, do you think it explains her sudden luck and obvious fame?"

"That's my theory." She replied. "But you didn't see the look on her face?"

"No, I was too busy avoiding it." He laughed. "Why?"

Artemis looked away for a bit and then she replied. "It's the same look she had the night before. The kind that sort of makes someone afraid of something."

Was it that clear? Was there really a look on Claire O Hara's face? Either way, there was one thing Jonathan could attest to just from being around Claire O' Hara, there was something like a malevolent force engulfing her completely. And if they weren't too careful, he feared that they too would be engulfed as well.

****

The Chez Panisse was founded in 1971 by a talented chef who put emphasis on the freshness and quality of ingredients, rather than technique. It boasted entirely of the famous California cuisine, with its locally sourced ingredients and delightful dishes such as Dungeness crab, smoked black cod and roasted lamb. The interior was done in warm woody shades and textures. It was truly a restaurant fit for the city locale, and it listed among its clientele famous French cuisine cook Julia Child, former president Bill Clinton, and director Francis Ford Coppola.

Claire couldn't believe she was dining at such a beautiful place with none other than Randy Fairbanks. The waiter showed them to the reserved seats up in the open roof dining floor. The floor had a very lovely view of the cityscape and the street below. They were seated and the menu was brought before them. Randy ordered roasted pork shoulder while Claire went for a smoked trout laced with lemons. They also ordered red wine. Claire tucked herself into her dinner and tasted it. It was delicious!

"So, tell me about yourself." Randy asked.

"Oh, I'm a student at UC-Berkeley, taking up fashion marketing." She replied. "I've always wanted to be a model. But I never got the opportunity...until recently, that is."

"Are you sure?" he asked. "No one ever gave you the break?"

"Yeah, they always said they wanted a girl with the...'it' factor." She replied.

"Those are amateurs." He said. "This is the big leagues. And if I may, you're quite pretty too. "

'Oh my God.' Claire thought. 'He actually called me pretty.' She felt her cheeks turn red and her heart beat with anticipation and joy. She still couldn't believe this was happening. 'It felt right alright.' She said to herself. All of this was right. She picked up a glass of wine and drank it. She noticed the ruby ring on her finger and slowly remembered the night at the crossroad. All of this success, this fame, it was her wish come true. She smiled, settled back into her seat and helped herself to more trout, while looking at the bustling street. She could see the cars pass by and people walking by, admiring the many window displays and taking photos.

Dining at an exclusive restaurant, at a seat reserved exclusively for her and Randy Fairbank, with a spectacular view; it was dining like royalty. And Claire reveled in it. The waiters would ask her what she would like to eat next or what she would like to drink. "Go ahead." Randy said. "Choose whatever you want. Tonight is the start of the rest of your life."

She smiled and began to order whatever she wanted. White sparkly champagne, luxurious chocolates, hotel bookings, everything.

As they waited on her, she suddenly heard the twinkling sound of bells in her ear. These were not the usual bells she would hear, nor were they the bells the waiters used. These were bells that one would hear on a collar, a jester's hat or even...wrist bells.

Claire looked around the floor to where the sound was coming from and then she saw her. Sitting a few tables away from where they were, covered in complete darkness, was the Lady on the Horse. Her white clothes looked almost slightly darker, and the veil that partially covered her face had small tattered edges and outlined her face. Claire could see a pointed chin and a pair of pale red lips looking at her. But what unnerved her the most was that she was looking straight at Claire with bright yellow eyes. Claire could see a set of bells on her wrists and toes. The Lady on the Horse was there.... following her?

No, it couldn't be the Lady on the Horse. She thought. She'd never come to a place like this. She called for a waiter and asked who the strange woman sitting in the far-off table was. The waiter looked at Claire with a confused look, and looked to where she was pointing. He turned back to face her and replied.

"I apologize, Miss Claire. But there is no one else here in the open roof floor." He replied.

"What?!" she turned to look at the table and still saw the strange Lady sitting at the table looking at her. "She's just there. Can't you see?"

The waiter looked at her again, let out a sigh and looked again. After a few seconds, he replied. "I'm sorry, Miss. But there is no one sitting at the table. Are you alright? Perhaps I can get you some water?"

"I'm telling you; she is there!" she said in a panic. "I can see her sitting right there, looking at me!"

"Perhaps you are full from enjoying our delicious selection." The waiter said. "Our customers have stated that after their meal, they might see things out of..."

"Are you saying I'm crazy?" Claire suddenly said, feeling both insulted and annoyed. "Are you calling me crazy?!"

"It's not like that, Miss." The waiter said. "I am saying that perhaps you are feeling ill and..."

"I'M NOT CRAZY OR SICK!" Claire bellowed, standing up and stamping her heeled feet onto the planked floor. "WHO THE HELL DO YOU THINK YOU ARE TALKING TO?"

"What is wrong with you?" Randy said, taking Claire's side and scolding the waiter. "She is not ill. Is this how you treat your customers? By insulting them?!"

The waiter tried to politely and calmly explain, but Randy and Claire had now reached the point where the manager was called to mediate things. As the manager persuaded Randy to calm down, Claire looked at the table and to her surprise, the Lady was gone. She rubbed her eyes again just to be sure she was seeing an empty table. Where did the lady go? Did she really imagine it?

Randy and Claire left the restaurant 30 minutes later and got into Randy's car. "I'm sorry that happened." Randy said, driving the car out of the parking lot. "You can be sure it won't happen again."

Claire said nothing as she stared at the ruby ring on her finger. Randy looked at her and added. "But I did reserve the entire floor just for us. I doubt there was anyone else here."

"I saw a woman." She stammered. "She-she-she was s-s-sitting in the t-t-t-table across ours. I c-c-c-could see her as plain as day."

Randy looked at her with the same confused look the waiter had given her. "Claire, I didn't see anyone else. Who did you see?"

"A woman....... a woman in white." She replied. She glanced at Randy. Fearful that he might think her mad, she quickly added. "I'm alright. I probably had too much to eat."

"That's alright." Randy said. "For a moment, I thought our date was ruined."

Date? The word seemed to echo in her mind. Did he just say 'our date'? She asked herself. "Our...date?" she repeated. Randy nodded and replied.

"Yes. Well, truth of the matter is...I like you, Claire. And I was wondering if I could see more of you." They reached the college dormitory and Randy stopped the car. "I just want to be sure you had a good time at least."

"Oh, I had a spectacular time." She replied. "It's been a really magical week and I don't want it to end at all."

Randy smiled, crawled over towards her and kissed her sweetly on her lips. "You are the luckiest girl in the world and I am the luckiest man to have you."

Claire let out a girlish giggle and got out of the car. She waved goodbye to Randy as he drove away. She felt so happy and excited, like a schoolgirl who had gotten her Christmas gifts a little earlier than everyone else. Who would have thought a beautiful, college girl would become an overnight wonder? She had lucrative contracts, more money and pretty things than any other girl and now, a famous celebrity for a boyfriend. Oh, it was too much for her to handle.

She walked to the steps of the dormitory and was about to enter the dorm, when she noticed the strange fog roll along the street. She heard the soft neigh of a large horse, and she turned around to see a familiar silhouette standing across the street, looking quite ominous.

Claire knew that silhouette. She had seen it not too long ago. She wondered why she was seeing her. What did she want? She stared at the silhouette as it slowly took the form of the Lady astride a large spectral white horse. The Lady looked at her before riding away once more into the fog. What did this mean? Claire brushed it off and went inside the dormitory, closing the door behind her. She looked at the ring, and for the first time since getting that ring, she began to feel a strange sense of dread.

Meanwhile, the staff at Chez Panisse had gathered around at the open roof dining floor and began to discuss what had happened earlier. It was the first time since opening that they had trouble with a regular customer. The manager then asked the waiter. "What happened? Why did Miss O'Hara lose her temper with you?

"She was asking me if I saw a woman sitting in the table over there." He replied pointing to the table. He then continued. "I told her that I did not see anyone, and I even told her that the floor had been reserved exclusively for her and Mr. Fairbanks."

"I heard him, Sir." Another waiter replied. "He simply asked and Miss O'Hara raised her tone with him."

"Was there anyone at all?" the manager asked.

The first waiter shook his head. "It was completely empty. We can even check the security cameras if you wish."

They then walked to the office where the security cameras were and checked the playback. And exactly as the waiter had spoken, the camera showed the entire floor empty, save for Randy Fairbanks and Claire O'Hara's table. "See?" he said. "There was no one else there." The camera also showed Claire suddenly looking frightened at the empty table and constantly staring at it while Randy argued with both manager and waiter.

"I think...Ms. O'Hara might be sick or something." The waiter said "She kept insisting that there was someone at the empty table."

"You're right." The manager said. "There's no one there. But she looks like she's frightened over it."

"Am I in trouble, Sir?" the waiter asked, gripping the sides on his vest. The manager shook his head, assuring him that he was perfectly alright. He kept looking at the camera playback, and for a while shook his head in disapproval.

"New celebrities. They can be annoying." He said. "Sometimes, I'd like to think there is a special place for them in hell."

****

"Are you alright?" Jonathan asked over the video call. He had decided to call Artemis and check on her. And in a way, it was a first for him. He had never tried calling a girl over the phone or a video call. But somehow, he liked this one girl. A whole lot. "I was just checking in."

"Are you sure it's not because you couldn't sleep that you're calling?" Artemis teased, adjusting her earphones and resting her head on her arms.

"N-No, I was really...really worried about you." Jonathan said folding his arms. She could see how Jonathan's cheeks turned slightly red, either from embarrassment or being called out for something else. She gave a girlish giggle and Jonathan couldn't help but laugh along with her. "Okay, I couldn't sleep."

"HA! I knew it!" she replied

"But I really wanted to see and check on you." He added. "I was worried that you might have gotten embarrassed or hurt by what your roommate said."

"Don't worry about it." Artemis said. "Truth be told. I'm kind of used to it. I mean, I'm not exactly pretty like her."

"No, I think you're beautiful." Jonathan said. "You're really pretty, especially when you put your hair up like now." He was referring to how her hair was tied in a nice neat ponytail.

"You think so?" Artemis said. "Well, you're not bad as well."

"You should meet my older brother then." He added. "He's a lot more handsome."

"I don't really go for looks; in case you haven't noticed" She said. "I'm more of a brains type." Jonathan kept his gaze on Artemis as they kept on talking. There was a sense of aesthete happiness inside Jonathan, as they talked more and more about other things such as school, family and the inevitability that their peers would know that they were friends. By and by, he could tell that Artemis was more than just a like-minded girl; she was the type that did not let other people's opinions about her matter. She was, in his mother's definition, a girl who marched to her own beat.

"Hey, I gotta go." Artemis said as they both heard the door unlock. "I think my pretty roommate is back. I'll call you in a bit, okay?"

"Yeah, sure..." Jonathan replied, feeling slightly sad that he had to cut the conversation so short. "I'll see you." And he ended the video call. In a way, he felt relieved that she was feeling better. But there was something else inside of him that felt something else. Something more...special and endearing.

Claire walked inside the dorm room and threw her keys and purse onto her bed, just as Artemis ended the call with Jonathan. "Oh, was that Jonathan?" Claire asked, eyeing Artemis with a teasing look.

"Yes, he just wanted to chat." She replied. "He couldn't sleep so..."

"He likes you. "Claire said, sitting on her bed and pulling her sandals out. "Only a guy who likes you would call you at this hour. Well, aren't you guys going to get serious?"

Artemis said nothing as she got up from her desk and began to prepare for bed. She had learned the futility of protesting with Claire; especially if Claire was convinced that she and Jonathan were more than just friends. In truth, perhaps she did feel something for Jonathan. She did like how he was polite and how they had the same affinity for music and the uncanny. But perhaps, what made him such an interesting person to be with was how he viewed her as someone of her own person.

"Hey," Claire suddenly said. "Can I ask you something?"

'That's a first,' Artemis thought as she buttoned up her pajamas. Claire was not one to ask her anything. In fact, she rarely interacted with Artemis in the shared room, unless it involved seeking Artemis's compliment on what she wore, or what she planned to do. "Don't you usually ask your friends if you have something on your mind?" Artemis asked.

"Let's say, they won't be much help with what's on my mind." Claire said. 'She's not one to dismiss her friends,' Artemis thought. This must be something that they wouldn't be able to understand. 'But why me?' She wondered. 'Why is Claire asking me?' Again, this was completely out of the norm for both of them. Artemis was the type that normally avoided anything that Claire would do or say to her. She just didn't have the energy for it.

However, this time was different. She could tell Claire had something rather serious on her mind. And she had a rather strange inclination as to what it was. She sighed and then asked. "Okay, you have my full attention. What is it?"

Claire let out a deep breath as if she had been mustering up the courage to say it. She sat on the edge of her bed and asked. "Do you believe in the Lady on the Horse?"

'That's what's on her mind?' Artemis thought, feeling a bit disappointed and silly. For a moment there, she was expecting something serious. But she saw the look in Claire's eyes and she knew what that look was. It was the same look she had when she woke up from the nightmare; the same look she had when she left earlier for her dinner date. It was the unmistakable look of fear.

Still, Artemis was a rational thinking girl. There was always logic behind something. She then replied. "You know I don't really think it's real. Why do you ask?"

"I.... I...well." Claire stammered and began to hesitate. "Well, let's say I'm asking for a friend."

Okay, let's go with that. Artemis said to herself, deciding to humor her. "Okay, what about your friend?"

"She completely believes it's real." Claire replied. "So much so that she actually played the ritual at a crossroad."

"And?"

"She tells me that a lady on a white horse appeared to her and asked her what her wish was." Claire continued. "She tells me she asked the lady to grant her fame and fortune."

"And what happened next?" Artemis asked, keeping her gaze focused entirely on Claire.

Claire replied. "The lady gave my friend a ring and then rode off. The next day, my friend started getting incredibly lucky and things have been great for me-I mean, her." She quickly corrected herself while at the same time, unconsciously began to twist a ring with a ruby stone around her finger.

Artemis noticed this, but did not say a word. "So that's a good thing for your friend. So why do you sound like you're worried about her?"

"She's...umm...worried that she's going crazy." Claire said quickly." She...she thinks she's seeing things and doesn't know why."

'Okay that is strange.' Artemis thought. 'Why was she seeing things? What were these things? "Did you-I mean your friend, ever ask what she was seeing?" Artemis asked.

"No." Claire said. "She didn't want to tell me because she thinks it will make her sound crazy." Artemis scratched her head thoughtfully and finally said.

"Okay, so as your friend's friend, what do you think it means? Do you think she's crazy?"

"I think...I think she's probably overwhelmed." Claire said. "I mean, if the Lady did come and give me-I mean my friend the ring and granted her wish, maybe she's still getting used to the whole success. Right?"

"Okay we can go with that. But- "Artemis looked at Claire's face intently. "Do you want my honest opinion on it?"

"Yes." She replied quickly without hesitation. Artemis then got up and after a brief moment of silence, looked at Claire and said. "I think your friend should be extra careful. There is no such thing as a free meal in this world. Everything comes with a price."

"What do you mean by, a price?"

"I don't know." Artemis then got into bed and added. "But you shouldn't worry. After all, it's not as if you played the game, right?"

"R-R-right." She stammered. "Well, since we don't know exactly I-I mean, my friend was seeing, then we can assume that nothing bad is going to happen to her."

Claire let out a sigh of relief and climbed into her own bed. "Thank you, Artemis. I'm glad we had the talk. I feel a whole lot better knowing that I-I mean, my friend will be alright."

"Glad I could help." Artemis replied as she groggily drifted off to sleep. Claire tucked herself in and pulled the sheets over her body. Nothing bad was going to happen. She told herself. The Lady won't harm me. After all, she granted my wish. I'm just scaring myself too much. Slowly, Claire closed her eyes and went to sleep.

****

As soon as he ended the call, Jonathan leaned back on his chair. He would have wanted to talk to her some more and even considered calling her back after a couple more minutes. But of course, it was a school night and she might have early morning classes. He took out his notebook and started working on his assignments when his roommate, Dick, came into the room once more, looking quite wasted, but still coherent.

"Studying again, Jonny boy?" he said with a slurred speech. "You're a Madden, you don't need to study."

"And you should be studying." Jonathan said, not looking up from his notebook. "If I remember correctly, you have an exam tomorrow and you can't afford to fail."

"Don't worry I'll wing it." He said. He then got up and sat in the desk next to Jonathan's and looked at him intently. Jonathan would write down on his notebook, completely ignoring the fact that Dick was staring at him with a rather teasing grimace. He would glance from time to time and still see the grinning Dick.

Finally, Jonathan laid his pen down and closed the notebook. He turned to face Dick, who was still grinning at him. "Alright, there's something on your mind." He said. "It's bothering you and it's bothering me. What is it?"

"I heard a little rumor going around the dormitory." He said. "The girl you had a coffee date with a few nights ago; I heard you asked her again."

"Do you people have anything better to do than talk about others?" Jonathan asked, giving Dick a rather stern and annoyed look. "Why are you so interested in the girl I'm seeing?"

"Because we all want to know the girl who is about to snag a Madden." Dick said. "We want to know what Artemis is like."

'So they know her name.' He thought grimly and sadly. 'He must have gotten it from Milo.' he thought. He sighed and said. "Artemis is a nice girl who just wants to get through college without any hijinks." He replied. "And how do you know her name?"

"I called in a favor." Dick said. "I asked the baristas at the college campus for the name of the girl you talk to often. It was easy. You're the only guy on campus who talks to the same girl in the same shop."

'I'm beginning to consider having coffee outside of campus.' Jonathan thought. At least Milo didn't tell him. "In any case," Jonathan began. "She is like me and she just wants to pass her exams."

"Come on my man, when are you going to ask her to date you?" Dick asked. "You're a Madden, you can have any girl you want. Heck, if I were you, I'd go and try to be friendly with her or even Claire O' Hara." Dick got up from his desk and jumped into his bed. "If I had it all, I'd be able to date Claire O' Hara. She's a major, dynamite babe."

"Why do you want to date someone like her?" he asked.

"Who wouldn't want to date someone like Claire?" Dick said while stretched out on the bed. "She's beautiful, popular, sexy, famous ...sexy..."

"Artemis is pretty. "Jonathan said, muttering under his breath. He suddenly realized that Dick heard his statement, as he noticed Dick looking at him again with that same grin.

"You like that girl, don't you? Admit it, Jonny boy!" he said. "You like that girl and you want to get freaky with her."

"You're a dick, you know that." Jonathan said as he glared at Dick before opening his notebook and resuming his schoolwork. "If you really want to get with Claire, why don't you try asking her out?"

"Okay, Jonny boy." Dick said. "Let's bet on it. If I ask Claire on a date and she says yes, you'll have to ask Artemis to be your girlfriend."

"And if Claire says no, you will leave me and Artemis alone." Jonathan said.

"Deal!" Dick said, holding his hand out to Jonathan. "Let's shake on it." It was better than making a deal with some alleged Lady on the Horse after all, Jonathan thought as he shook hands with Dick. Dick then drifted off to sleep, obviously exhausted from whatever party or activity he attended.

Finally, Jonathan thought. Some peace and quiet. He went about working on his homework before yawning and deciding to go to bed. He got into bed and tucked himself in, his lingering thoughts entirely on Artemis's smile. "Good night, Artemis." He said to himself, slowly closing his eyes.

<u>Chapter 7</u>

"I'm telling you, today is the start of the rest of your life." A man dressed in a navy button down shirt and slacks said, as Claire signed her name on several contracts in his office. Sitting on her right was Randy Fairbanks, and on the other side was her new manager, Ellen. This man was none other than Mr. Albert Cohen, the city's highest paid movie producer. And the contracts Claire was signing were for big budget Hollywood films; some of which, by the looks of it were sure fire candidates for Awards nominations.

"Let me tell you, when Ellen here said you were a natural talent, I was skeptic at first." Mr. Cohen said. "But, after seeing you and your portfolio, I'm a believer. And to think you're still in college."

"Well, I guess I'm just born lucky." Claire said as she signed the last contract. "So, what's next?"

Mr. Cohen gathered the signed contracts and flipped through them. "Basically, I tell you how much you earn, what your contract entitles you, and your benefits and dues." He began to enumerate exactly what he said, from the benefits, to rules, to how much Claire would be earning as royalty. Upon hearing the amount, she almost felt like she was at a loss for words. She never expected to be earning that much. And per day too, no less. Even more so when screening occurred.

"That's a lot." She said.

"And you deserve it." Her manager Ellen said. "You are a certified overnight sensation." Even Randy held her hand and gave her an assuring look of approval. "From now on, things are going to be a whole lot better for you."

And true to her manager's word, Claire would experience what most people would call a fairy tale come true. She was being driven around in limousines and expensive cars, having dinners in expensive and exclusive restaurants, and going on luxurious and exotic dates with Randy Fairbanks, who at this time, was now confirmed to be dating her. She was even receiving beautiful jewels, furs, designer clothes, shoes, bags, everything. She was, without question, the luckiest girl in the city. No, the world.

And she was having it all. The fame, the fortune. The things. The man. She had come a long way from going to frat parties, sleeping around and endless shopping. Hell, she even got over her childish crush and ambition of dating a Madden. How could a Madden compare to the prestige and notoriety commanded by Randy Fairbanks? She relished in the abundance of all and for the first time, she wanted more. She didn't want this to end.

And yet, she was still going to college. Most people would find that admirable in an overnight sensation's repertoire. Not only would she be talented, she would also be considered a role model for aspiring ladies like herself. At least, that is what she wanted everyone else to think.

To say that Claire was doing it for the sake of image would be an understatement. She wanted to command the notoriety and prestige that the older Madden had once had. What was fame worth if she couldn't conquer even the college? Even if it meant staying in the same dormitory with a no nonsense, unattractive girl like Artemis Rosi.

"You know, Artemis." She began as she spread some cold cream on her face. "You can be beautiful if you just follow my now patented beauty regimen."

"If I wanted to look like some marble faced person, I would." Artemis said sarcastically. "Besides, you know the whole beauty thing is in the eye of the beholder."

"Come on, Artemis. Don't be such a wet blanket." Claire said. "You're really a looker. Hey, that gives me an idea." She got up and took Artemis by the wrist. "You're going to be my new pet project."

"What?!" Artemis asked in an annoyed tone. "Claire, I'm sorry, but I'm not some project or experiment."

"Don't you want Jonathan to ask you out again?" she asked in a teasing tone. "I heard from the grapevine that he likes you a lot. Come on, Artemis. Everybody wants to be me. Beautiful. Popular. Desirable."

"Not interested." Artemis said, putting her foot down on the subject matter. Not that she was curious as to whether what Claire said was true, but it was more of she didn't really care for things like that. She decided to change the subject. "So, did you talk to your friend about her problem?"

"What friend's problem?" Claire asked. "Oh, you mean 'that problem.'" She knew what Artemis was asking about.

She wondered why Artemis was even asking about that. It was almost two months since she indirectly told Artemis about what she had seen or witnessed. And thanks to Artemis's advice, if any rational thinking person would call it advice, Claire had been feeling a lot better and more productive than before.

She reached for her hand where the ruby ring was, and unconsciously turned it around her finger. She had, without her own knowledge, developed a calming habit of turning the ring around her finger whenever she spoke or thought about the Lady. She didn't want to admit it to anyone, not even to herself. But despite having a smug air of confidence and haughtiness, there was a burning question that constantly kept her on edge.

She asked the Lady to grant her wish of fame, fortune and notoriety. But not once had she considered what the lady wanted in return, if there was any even. Nothing was free in this world, that much was a given. Still, it had been a while since she last had any encounters with the sight of the Lady.

Perhaps it was Artemis's silly way of saying she was jealous. She thought. That could be it. After all, nothing bad had happened. And if this streak of luck and fortune were to last, all she had to do was dwell on that.

"That's good." Artemis replied. "And is she being careful?"

"Why should she?" Claire asked, her tone rising a bit. "Nothing bad has happened to me-I mean, to her. She was probably being overwhelmed."

"If...'your friend' played the game and summoned the Lady just as you said, you should know she's dealing with things that we have no control of." She said. "That alone is scary and she should be careful. You have to tell her to be careful."

"Look, nothing has happened so far." Claire said. "So, she's alright. Now..." She got up and carried a face towel. "I'm going to wash my face and go on a date with my boyfriend, Randy." And she walked to the bathroom and closed the door behind her.

Why should I be careful? Claire thought as she walked to the bathroom's sink. She looked at her cream covered reflection in the mirror, and turned on the sink's faucet to scoop up some water in her hands. 'I haven't seen the Lady in a while and maybe I wasn't seeing her'. She splashed some water unto her face and gently wiped it with her towel. She scooped another handful and was splashing it on her face when she suddenly felt the air around her thicken.

She felt a weird and heavy atmosphere envelope her, as she closed her eyes and lifted her face up to wipe it. Slowly, she opened her eyes and gasped at what she saw in the mirror. "No...it can't be..." she said under her breath, a twinge of fear in her tone.

Looking straight at her was not her reflection, but another face. Draped entirely in white with only half the face visible through a covered and torn looking veil, the woman had eyes as yellow as a hawk, and a gaze so deep and frightening, as though it were that of a predator stalking its prey. Claire recognized this face; she had seen it multiple times. It was her.

"Are you happy?" She heard the woman speak beneath the covered veil. "Have you gotten everything that your heart desired?"

"I...I..." She was speechless, she didn't know what to say or even respond to that. She was petrified at the sight of the Lady looking back at her. Dare she answer the lady? Before she could say anything, the room started to grow dark and cold. So cold that she could even see her own breath escape from her lips.

She looked at the mirror and saw her own reflection; only this time, it looked distorted. She could see her fair skin slowly turn grey and shrivel, as though all the blood were being drained from it.

Her eyes were jaundiced and dull, and her hair hung loosely on her scalp, its luster slowly diminishing and turning grey with age. She couldn't believe it! Her reflection was withering and aging with fear.

She suddenly saw long, bony fingers slowly crawl up behind her ears towards her hair. She could feel each digit grasp her skull and she instinctively reached behind to feel a pair of withered hands. Not wanting to alarm herself and Artemis outside, she took a deep breath and slowly turned her head to face whatever was behind her.

She could see the veiled head of the Lady behind her, her face lowered and obscured by the layers of the now stained white cloth. Claire began to let out panicked breaths, as the Lady slowly raised her head to reveal her face. Her eyes widened with fear as she could now see the Lady's features.

Before Claire could say anything, the Lady opened her mouth and let out a guttural growl and said ominously. "I come again...to take my due...." She then let out an unearthly scream that made the entire room shake. Claire screamed in complete horror as the Lady's fingers slowly squeezed on her scalp.

"NO! NO!" Claire screamed over and over again. "WHAT DO YOU WANT!?" She cried out and closed her eyes. "WHAT DO YOU WANT? WHAT DO YOU WANT?!"

"What's going on in here?!" The bathroom door had burst open and Artemis walked inside. "Claire, what in the world?"

****

Artemis was no fool. She could tell that there was something bothering Claire for the past couple of months. Although Claire was capable of hiding it, her roommate saw through her façade. And now, her suspicions were fully confirmed when she heard Claire screaming from inside the bathroom. Artemis bolted out of her chair and tried to open the door.

Locked. She thought, as she tried to pry the door open. She kept hearing Claire scream inside. "Hang on Claire!" she called out, using her body as a battering ram to push the door open. She then took a deep breath and kicked at the door. The hinges came undone and Artemis pushed it open.

"Claire?" She called out, walking inside. She stopped and saw Claire lying on the floor, curled up in a quivering fetal position. She was grasping her scalp and shaking. "Claire, are you alright?" Artemis asked, dropping to her knees and placing a hand on her shoulders. "Claire?"

As soon as Artemis' hand touched her shoulder, Claire's gaze focused on Artemis and she suddenly slapped her hand away. "DON'T TOUCH ME! DON'T TOUCH ME!" She cried out.

"Claire, it's me. Artemis." She said, holding Claire by the shoulders. "Calm down. It's alright. It's alright." She could see the frantic look in her eyes as she tried to calm Claire down. But Claire kept on screaming and thrashing about on the bathroom floor.

There was only thing she could do. "Come on Claire, let's get you up and get you some water." She said, as she carefully helped Claire up. Holding her with both hands, Artemis guided Claire into their shared room and gently set her down on her bed. She had somehow managed to calm Claire down and even got her to drink some water. "Are you feeling better?" she asked.

Claire feebly nodded and then said. "I saw...I saw..."

"You saw what?" Artemis asked.

Before she could say anything, Claire's phone rang. She picked it up and completely ignoring Artemis' question, she answered the phone. Her expression immediately lightened up as though nothing had happened. She smiled and hung up. "Ah it was nothing." She finally replied. "Umm, I thought I saw a ...a roach."

"That didn't sound like someone who screamed just because of a roach." Artemis said. "Are you sure you're okay?"

"Yeah, I'm fine, thank you." Claire said, raising her tone a bit. "Look, I'm going to be late for a shooting. I have to go." Claire quickly changed into her clothes and walked out of the dorm room. Artemis watched through the window as Claire walked to the car waiting by the street and got inside. She sat inside and as the door closed, Artemis gasped at what she suddenly saw. She closed the window and took a step back. She reached for her phone and called the one person she could turn to.

"Pickup...pick up...hello, Jonathan? Hey hi...ummm... Listen, think you can meet me at my dorm like right now? I'm changing and uh...think you can bring your scooter along? Well...listen ...um.... you won't believe it, but."

She took another deep breath and said. "I think I saw the Lady. Where? How? I don't know how, it's a long story. But I think Claire's in trouble. Why do I say this? I saw the Lady in Claire's car."

On a normal night, Jonathan would usually spend it simply staying inside his room and watching some videos online. Perhaps play a couple of games or even listen to some more of Dave Navarro's music. Either that or read some more books by his favorite authors and try his hand at writing. He never expected to get a call from Artemis sounding quite frantic. Nor did he expect to hear her ask him to come over to her dorm with his scooter.

"Why do you want me there?" he would say. "Is everything alright?" He listened as she paused over the phone before finally revealing something quite...unusual. "What do you mean, you saw the Lady?" He asked again as he pulled his jacket out of the closet and grabbed his keys. "What do you mean 'Claire's in trouble'? Okay, hang on. I'll be there in a bit."

He quickly ended the call and made his way to the door only to bump into Dick. "Hey, sorry I gotta go." Jonathan said.

"Where are you heading, Jonny boy?" Dick asked. "It's not like you to go out at night."

"I'm heading over to Artemis' dorm." He replied. "Now, come on man. Let me through."

"Aww man, I knew it!" Dick exclaimed. "I knew you like that girl so much. This is a classic booty call."

"Geez, Dick. Why do you have to think with your dick?" Jonathan said. "Look, I don't have time to argue. I need to go. Now get out of my way." He brushed Dick aside and walked through the door and out into the parking lot. He got on his scooter and sped off towards the girls' dormitory.

He found Artemis anxiously waiting by the curbside. He had never seen her look as worried. "Okay, I'm here." He said handing her the spare helmet. "What's gotten you all riled up?" Artemis fastened the helmet on her head and got behind Jonathan.

"We have to go to Claire's shooting location." Artemis said. "Come on." She reached over and held Jonathan by the waist. Jonathan felt, for lack of a better description, tingly and nice when Artemis held him by the waist. He revved up his scooter and both of them sped along the busy street past several buildings and shops.

"You didn't answer my question earlier." Jonathan said as they reached a stop light. "What do you mean by, you saw the Lady and that Claire is in trouble?"

Artemis quickly explained what Claire had told her months before. "She said that she's been seeing the Lady, but she keeps on avoiding it when I ask her why she says this." She said. "Then only a few minutes ago, she started to scream inside our bathroom. I walked in and I saw her so terrified, but she just brushed it off."

"She's hiding something alright." Jonathan said as they resumed the drive.

"And when she was heading out, I watched her get into the car and I saw a lady dressed in white sitting next to her inside."

"What?!" Jonathan exclaimed, stopping the scooter abruptly. "You saw a lady dressed in white in her car? Are you saying it's the Lady on the Horse?"

Artemis nodded. "Jonathan, we have to get to the location. I think something bad is going to happen."

"Hang on." Jonathan sped the scooter up and like a racer, weaved in and out of the traffic filled streets. 'It may be a wild goose chase.' he thought. But there was no mistaking the look in Artemis' eyes. After all, he'd had that look when he saw the Lady in the library.

They approached a city block that had been closed off to the public. This was the location of the new action thriller film that would star Randy Fairbanks and his girlfriend, the overnight sensation, Claire O' Hara. Jonathan parked the scooter at a nearby lot and both he and Artemis made their way towards the set. "Where do you think Claire is?" Artemis asked.

"Most likely in a trailer or on set." Jonathan said. "Look, over there." He pointed to where a crowd had gathered. "She's probably over there." They walked towards the crowd and after weaving in and out, came across a barricaded set where the crew were filming a scene. In the center stood the film's stars, Randy and Claire, dressed in full costume. The director was now bellowing instructions.

"Okay, Claire. This is the scene where you must drop your gun slowly and run to his arms." He said. "Alright?"

They watched as the two leads acted out their respective scenes without do overs. The director then called for a break in order to review the footage. Jonathan and Artemis saw Claire walking towards her tent. Artemis quickly called out. "Claire! Claire, wait!"

She was suddenly stopped by a large, burly man in a black shirt. "Get back over the line, missy." He said, pointing to where there was a barricaded fence. "No civilians allowed."

"Hey buddy, we need to speak to Claire O' Hara." Jonathan said. "We don't want any trouble. Just let us have a few minutes with her."

"Get back over the line." The man repeated, cracking his knuckles in a threatening manner. Jonathan and Artemis flinched for a moment, but both stood their ground.

"Just give us ten minutes with her." Jonathan said. "It's important."

"Yeah, I get you." The man replied sarcastically. "Look buddy, if you want to meet Ms. O'Hara, you'll have to get a VIP pass. Now, get lost."

"What's going on?" Claire had walked towards the man flanked by two assistants. "What's with the noise-Oh, Artemis and Jonathan? What are you doing here?"

"You know these two, Ms. O'Hara?" the man asked.

"Yes, they're schoolmates of mine." She replied.

"Claire, we need to talk to you." Artemis said. "It's really important."

"You can let them through, Bob." Claire said. "I can spare maybe fifteen minutes."

The man nodded and grunting at Jonathan and Artemis, stepped aside and cast them angry glares, as he allowed the two to walk in. Artemis approached Claire and said. "Claire, can we talk in private?"

"I'm on break and we can talk in my tent." She replied, not sure why they wanted to talk to her. More importantly, why they were here together. They walked to her tent where Claire was immediately waited on by stylists and assistants. "This is a surprise, why are you both here?"

"Claire, you need to tell us what you saw earlier." Artemis said, not waiting to beat around the bush.

"What are you talking about?" Claire asked defensively.

"Artemis tells me you screamed like something terrible was happening. "Jonathan said. "And to be honest, you seem to be on edge."

"On edge?" she repeated. "What makes you think I'm on edge? I'm going places. I'm on top of the world. I'm getting famous."

"Exactly." Jonathan said. "Let's be real. Don't you find it odd that all of this is happening like snap?"

"That means I'm a natural talent and everything is going my way." She said stubbornly. She then eyed them suspiciously and added. "What is this about, really? Are you...jealous? "

"What?" They both repeated. Claire continued.

"Are you jealous of my fame? Are you upset Jonathan that you're not dating me? Is that it? Are you jealous of my beauty, Artemis?"

"God, you're so full of yourself." Artemis said. "What makes you think I'm jealous of you?"

"Well then why are you here, raining on my happiness?"

"Because she's worried about you." Jonathan said, raising his tone a bit. "she saw something strange ride with you in the car earlier." He stopped for a moment as they both stared at Claire's confused look. He wondered if he had spoken too soon. Maybe Claire might think they were crazy.

Claire looked at them and began to laugh. "Wow, you saw something strange? That's funny. I never pegged either of you to be jokesters."

"Just tell us what you saw." Jonathan said. At that exact moment, the director called for the cast to return to the scene for another shoot. Bob the security guard approached them and said. "Ms. O'Hara, they are calling all the actors back. Shall I escort these two back behind the line?"

"You may, Bob." Claire said. "We just finished talking for now."

"You heard the lady. "Bob said, placing a hand on both Jonathan and Artemis. "Let's go!"

"Claire, what exactly did you see?" Jonathan cried out as he and Artemis were escorted out of the tent and back to the line.

Claire did not look back as the make-up artists began to apply make up to her face. She didn't understand why they had to come all this way to badger her on what she saw. 'Why should they know? It was nothing after all.' She thought to herself, as she walked back to the set. Nothing at all.

The director watched through his film lenses as Claire and Randy acted out their parts once more. The crowd that had gathered behind the set watched in awe, as Randy and Claire gave an outstanding performance. And when they paused in between, Claire could hear, albeit from the distance, the 'oohs' and 'aahs' that came from the crowd.

These were admirers who had gone out of their way to see her perform. To see her and adore her. She could see them waving at her, crying out her name in adoration. All eyes were on her after all. She then saw Jonathan and Artemis just looking at her with a rather different expression. Why weren't they admiring her?

"Okay, Claire." The director's voice cut through her thoughts. "In this scene, you will see a shape appear out of the mist right there." He pointed to the spot where several stagehands were operating a fog machine from behind one of the houses. "You must slowly walk towards it and call out the name. You are now hallucinating the retreating figure of Randy, alright?"

"Alright." She nodded as she walked towards the spot.

"ACTION!" The director called out. Claire slowly approached the spot and watched as the fog slowly began to build up. She waited for the supposed shape to appear. She could see what she assumed was the shape she had to call out to. She took a deep breath and said her line.

"Joe? Joe is that you?" She ran towards the shape. "Is it you, my darling?" She began to notice that the fog was getting thicker and thicker. 'Wow.' she thought. 'The crew is really going all out with the fog machine.' Slowly, she noticed that the buildings were vanishing into the thick fog as she walked around.

'Wow, they're really going all out.' She thought, hiding the fact that she felt a bit uneasy with the thick fog, and the feeling of being all by herself. She walked further on, still sure that this was all part of the scene.

Probably getting a genuine reaction was what the director wanted. She thought. She walked on further until her foot suddenly hit something and she tripped onto the street. "Ouch!" she exclaimed as her skin grazed on the rough asphalt road. "Oh my god! I'm sorry, Director." She called out, looking over her shoulder. She saw that she couldn't see the director or the staff and crew.

She sat up straight and looked at her knee. There was a very large and nasty bruise on her knee. "Great." She muttered. "This is just great. Hello?!" She called out again. "Ellen? Director? Are we still rolling?"

Silence. She suddenly felt the air grow cold and thick, and the feeling of being all by herself was starting to slowly creep in. The director really wants me to act, she thought. It's not funny. Suddenly, she heard the sound of bells tinkling in the air and the familiar sound of hooves trotting forward. She remembered this sound and saw the fog slowly lift away. She gasped in horror as she found herself standing at the center of the crossroads!

How in the world did she end up at the crossroads!? She looked around and saw that she was still covered in the same fog as that night. There were no buildings or shops or even simple sounds. Save for the tinkling bells and the approaching hooves. She then saw the shape of the Lady on the Horse appear before her. But there was something different about the Lady and her horse. Something she found…utterly terrifying.

The large white horse that had once been as pure and majestic now had dark red menacing eyes and looked slightly emaciated; its fine trusses of white and blonde hair was thinning and hung loose on its head. The fine jeweled saddle now looked withered and had a few jewels plucked out. The Lady herself was now dressed in dirty white robes with tatters at the edges. Her feet and hands were now bony, with the skin slightly grey and stretched tightly. Her face was still covered with a veil, but instead of beautiful amber yellow eyes, bloodshot, red eyes could be seen beneath the layers of cloth.

Claire took a step back as the Lady drew near. "Are you satisfied?" The Lady asked in a low and ethereal voice. "You are now famous and now everyone will know your name...."

"Yes. But I want more." Claire said. "I want them to love me and adore me. I want it all..."

The Lady on the Horse began to draw near and Claire slowly stepped back again. The Lady stretched her hand out and said. "I have come for the due. The ring....and...you."

You? What did she mean by that? Did she mean... me!? Did she come...to take me?! Claire suddenly felt her heart beat rapidly as she turned on her heels and ran away. She looked over her shoulder as she heard the galloping sound of horse hooves coming after her, the Lady riding furiously and intently. The wind began to blow her many layered veils off her head and Claire would finally see the enigmatic face of the Lady on the Horse.

She had never seen such a frightening face. Skeletal and grotesque! Claire kept running and running not caring in the world where she was headed. She just wanted to get away from the Lady. She would glance at the red ring on her finger and she tried desperately to pull it out. But for some reason, it was stuck on her finger. As she ran, she started to remember exactly what Artemis had said a few months ago. 'Nothing is free. Everything had a price.' She would stumble and crawl on the ground as the Lady drew nearer and nearer.

She stopped in the middle of a road and tried to frantically pull the ring out of her finger. She saw the Lady on the Horse stop a few feet away from her. Claire looked up and cried out. "WHAT DO YOU WANT FROM ME!?"

The Lady looked at her and replied. "Payment for your wish."

"I can pay you." Claire said, frantically tugging at her wish. "Name your price. I can afford it."

The Lady just stared at her and softly, but ominously replied. "You can't put a price on your soul…"

At that moment, Claire heard Artemis and Jonathan's voices calling out to her. She looked to the direction of their voices and saw two bright orbs of light coming towards her at an incredible pace.

"CLAIRE, LOOK OUT! GET OUT OF THE ROAD!" Were the last words Claire O'Hara heard, when a charging force struck her and her body fell limp against the asphalt road.

The fog slowly lifted and Claire could faintly see the crowd gathered behind several of the film's security team as people screamed and panicked. She could see her hand lying limp and stiff in front of her; the ruby ring completely gone. Slowly, she closed her eyes and let out her last breath of life.

****

Jonathan and Artemis were pushed back into the crowd by Bob the security guard. They were going to film the crucial scene where Claire's character runs into the fog, the crew told the crowd. Jonathan and Artemis watched as Claire walked to the director's chair and got her instructions. She would then walk towards the fog covered scene and act her role.

They saw her perform. 'She was really good.' he thought. "I have to hand it to her." He whispered to Artemis. "If she wasn't all about herself, she's actually good."

"I still feel that something's not right." Artemis whispered back to him. "I can see it in her eyes."

They then heard the director call out to Claire to move. But it seemed that Claire was too far away. How odd. Jonathan thought. Why wasn't Claire moving or listening?

To the crowd's surprise, they started to see Claire pacing back and forth in the fog and muttering and mumbling to herself. They saw her trip and fall to the ground and crawl and get up. Was that part of the script? Or was she improvising?

Jonathan noticed how thick the fog had become. He noticed the security guards watching and they too, seemed both impressed and confused. He then heard a member of the film crew whisper to one other member. "Is it just me or is the fog a little too thick?"

"Yeah, I thought so too. Did the Director change his mind on the fog thickness?"

"Either way, that doesn't look natural to me."

'Doesn't look natural.' He repeated the phrase in his mind as he looked at Artemis' face. She too had noticed it and like Jonathan, felt that something was off. Suddenly they heard Claire screaming in the fog. It didn't sound like a rehearsed scream. The crew began to marvel at how realistic it sounded. But somehow, it didn't feel right.

They then saw Claire frantically running towards the crowd with a frantic and bewildered look in her eye. They would see her looking over her shoulder while reaching for a ring on her finger. "What's gotten into her?" They heard the director speak. "That's not in the script!"

Randy had emerged from his tent and saw Claire frantically running and crawling on the ground as though trying to get away from something. "Claire." He said, running to her and holding her by the shoulders. "What is it? What's wrong?"

He was met with a guttural and bellowing cry, and a frantic look of fear in her eyes as she pushed him away and ran through the crowd. The security guards tried to stop her, but she had managed to push them off as well.

Grabbing her hand, Jonathan and Artemis maneuvered through the now panic-stricken crowd and tried to catch up to her. "What's happening to her?" Artemis asked.

"I'm not sure." Jonathan said. "But she looks spooked. Like something was coming after her." They ran after her fleeing figure. They could tell she was quite scared and suddenly noticed where she was headed. She was heading out of the closed block and into the streets. "CLAIRE! CLAIRE! CLAIRE!" Artemis called out. "CLAIRE STOP! LET US HELP YOU!"

They heard her panic and cry out. "WHAT DO YOU WANT FROM ME?! I CAN PAY YOU!" Pay you? What did she mean by that? Jonathan wondered. He could hear the crowd behind following, as though to see where Claire was headed. They finally stopped as they saw Claire standing in the middle of the road, muttering frantically. "I can pay...name your price..."

"Claire!" Jonathan called out. "Claire!"

They suddenly heard the sound of a truck horn coming towards her and both Artemis and Jonathan cried out. "CLAIRE LOOK OUT, GET OUT THE ROAD!" They tried to get her out of the way, but it was too late. The truck had run over Claire in an instant, tossing her body in the air and letting it fall limp into the street.

Artemis gasped in horror as Jonathan covered her eyes upon the sight of the impact. They could see the crowd slowly gather around, and there were sounds of panic and screams that echoed all over the street. 'How could this have happened?' Jonathan thought. 'What just happened?' He looked around the crowd and at Claire's limp and lifeless body, before suddenly seeing something...truly strange.

"Artemis." He said in a low whisper. "Look." He gestured across the street. Artemis looked up and saw where he was pointing. She gasped.

Standing across the street was the faint and mangled figure of Claire O' Hara's, her eyes looking hopeless and in utter despair; wearing her bloodstained dress. Beside her was a large white spectral horse that was majestic and beautiful. Sitting astride the horse was a lady dressed in layers of beautiful soft, white silk with gold trimmings and jewels. Her face was covered with a veil save for her eyes which were a beautiful amber yellow. On her feet were bells attached to her shoes and anklets and on her fingers were numerous rings; one of which was the ruby ring that Claire had.

Jonathan and Artemis couldn't believe what they were seeing; it was the Lady on the Horse. The Lady then flicked the reigns of her horse's muzzle and began to ride away gently with Claire walking in tow, a look of sorrow as she followed. She took one last glance at Jonathan and Artemis and began to mouth the words. "Help....me...." before she and the Lady disappeared into the fog.

"What-what did we just see?" Artemis asked, stammering in complete disbelief.

"I...I...I ..." For the first time, Jonathan didn't know how to answer. "I...I... don't know." He stuttered. "But...I don't think this is the end of it...."

UNLOCKABLES

Congrats on achieving a milestone! (getting to the end of this book).
For that, you get a chance to enjoy another BadCreative book.
Support your local publisher by grabbing another amazing, novel on
offer
>>> here <<<US
>>> here <<< UK
>>> here <<< FR
>>> here <<< DE

>>> here <<< and >>> here <<<

Thank you for purchasing, and don't forget to drop us a review on our Amazon page.
#TheCrossing